Tales of Trenzalore

DOCTOR WHO

Tales of Trenzalore

Tales of Trenzalore *collects four of the Doctor's adventures*
from different periods during the Seige of Trenzalore and the
ensuing battle:

'Let It Snow' *by Justin Richards*
'An Apple a Day' *by George Mann*
'Strangers in the Outland' *by Paul Finch*
'The Dreaming' *by Mark Morris*

BBC
BOOKS

1 3 5 7 9 10 8 6 4 2

Published as an ebook in 2014 by BBC Books, an imprint of Ebury Publishing.
A Random House Group Company

This paperback edition published in 2014

Doctor Who is a BBC Wales production for BBC One.
Executive producers: Steven Moffat and Brian Minchin

The Random House Group Limited Reg. No. 954009

Addresses for companies within the Random House Group
can be found at www.randomhouse.co.uk

A CIP catalogue record for this book is available from the British Library.

ISBN 978 1 849 90844 3

Editorial director: Albert DePetrillo
Series consultant: Justin Richards
Project editor: Steve Tribe
Cover design: Lee Binding © Woodlands Books Ltd, 2014
Production: Alex Goddard

Printed and bound in the USA

To buy books by your favourite authors and register for offers,
visit www.randomhouse.co.uk

Contents

Tales of Trenzalore

As it had been foretold, the armies of the universe gathered at Trenzalore. Only one thing stood between the planet and destruction – the Doctor. Only one thing stood between the Doctor and the next Great Time War – his name. For nine hundred years, he defended the planet and the tiny town of Christmas against the forces that would destroy it.

Behind the technology barrier maintained by the Church of the Papal Mainframe, at the heart of the Truth Field, close to the crack between this universe and the next, the Doctor stood steadfast between life and death. He never knew how long he could keep the peace. He never knew what creatures would emerge from the snowy night to threaten him next. He knew only that at the end he would die on Trenzalore.

Some of what happened during those terrible years is well documented. But most of it has remained shrouded in mystery and darkness.

Until now…

Brought together in this volume are just four incidents from the time the Doctor spent on Trenzalore.

Four stories of heroism and danger. Four stories that document the lengths the Doctor would go to in order to protect the place he had made his home. Four out of hundreds – perhaps thousands.

Over time, more stories will surely emerge about how the Doctor protected the town of Christmas, and how the townsfolk took him to their heart and cherished the time he bought them. But for the moment, we have only rumours and legends, myths and stories.

Tales of Trenzalore…

Let It Snow

by Justin Richards

Chapter 1

The sky burned. Crantle was used to the lights that punctuated the long nights – the stars and the countless spaceships that orbited Trenzalore and had done since before his grandfather was born. But this was something different. A trail of fire blazing across the heavens and crashing down on the other side of the high ridge that surrounded the town of Christmas.

Crantle lived outside the main community. He did the snow run – taking sleds laden with snow to the outlying communities. The snow farm at Christmas was the main source of water for many of the further settlements on Trenzalore. Crantle harvested the snow, packing it into the insulated holds of his sleds. They travelled in a small convoy, Crantle in the lead sled, calling to the dogs, though they knew the route as well as he did. The other sleds followed, roped loosely together, speeding over the frozen ground.

When the snow gave way to ice, and the ice slowly gave way to a greener landscape, Crantle lowered wheels beneath the sleds to continue on into the almost perpetual night. A round trip took him over a week.

Over a week with no company except the dogs and his own tuneless singing. It would have driven some men insane, but Crantle loved every minute of it.

He spent the time between trips looking after the dogs, and tending the small heat-houses where he grew his own vegetables – anything that lessened his dependence on others. Meat and fruit he got in return for the snow he traded.

He wasn't due to make another snow run for several days yet, so the burning sky was a curious distraction. Crantle sat in his favourite wooden chair on the front porch, and watched the trail of fire blistering past the stars and distant ships. It disappeared behind the ridge in a sudden shower of sparks. In the depths of the night, two more lines of fire etched a path towards the planet. But Crantle didn't notice them. His attention was on the dying glow where the first fireball had fallen.

'Meteor' was a name somewhere at the back of his memory. A rock falling from the sky. One of the communities that Crantle dealt with was a small mining town. They dug into the ground – into rock – looking for valuable minerals and ores. Perhaps Crantle didn't need to bother digging. Perhaps the rock he'd seen fall had shattered, showering valuable debris across the landscape. It was unlikely, Crantle thought, but as he had nothing better to do it was worth a look. He lived close to the top of the ridge, so it was probably less than an hour's walk. Even if it wasn't valuable, it might be interesting.

The light from the twin moons of Trenzalore revealed a blackened scar across the snow that was a reversal of the trail of fire across the sky. Snow was already covering the burned ground again, the flakes hissing and melting where they fell onto the hotter patches. Crantle walked beside the bare ground, using it as a path to guide him to the meteor, testing the snow ahead of him with his long wooden staff. He could just make out the jagged dark shape of the meteor nudged up against the edge of a wooded area.

The moon-pine trees swayed gently in the cool breeze, waiting patiently for the few minutes of daylight that would sustain them through the next long night. Crantle peered into the moonlight shadows, half expecting to see the gangly shape of the Doctor waiting for him among the trees. If anyone from Christmas came to see what had fallen beyond the ridge, it would be the Doctor. If there was anyone in Christmas that Crantle actually enjoyed talking to, it was the Doctor. There was something about the man that engendered confidence. Somehow Crantle felt he could be alone with the Doctor – there would be no prying, no polite questions, no pointless conversation simply for the sake of it.

But as he reached the end of the charred path through the snow, Crantle saw no one. In front of him, the meteor was smoking as if it was still on fire. Its jagged side glistened in the moonlight, steaming, melting. Water pooled round the base of it, running back down the wound it had gouged out of the ground. It was about twice Crantle's height, and as deep – a rough sphere rounded by the heat of its arrival. And, to Crantle's surprise, it was made of ice. As he approached, it wasn't heat that he felt on his face, but a cold chill.

Crantle prodded at the ice with his wooden staff.

Stepping closer, he reached out a tentative hand, patting the side of the ice. He could feel the chill through the thick padding of his glove. But something else too – a faint juddering, a vibration. As if the ice was shivering from its own cold. He wiped his glove across it, clearing the frost and leaving a smooth, glassy surface. It reflected the moons and the stars, their light smeared and distorted on the undulating surface.

But beneath the shimmering lights, deep within the ice itself, there was another shape – dark and blurred. A figure? Shuddering, as if it was struggling to move within its icy tomb. A trick of the moonlight, Crantle thought. No one could survive inside a block of ice. And this ice had fallen from the sky – no one could be inside it.

The sound was like a tree snapping in the wind. A sudden crack, and the whole section of ice in front of Crantle split from top to bottom. A section sheared off, crashing to the ground and shattering like glass. Instinctively, he stepped back. Moments later, a fist punched through the ice close to where his head had been. Sharp, transparent splinters whipped past Crantle's face, stinging his cheeks and catching in his beard.

If he cried out in surprise or fear, the sound was lost in the explosion of ice as the creature inside shattered its way out and stood before him. A massive figure, towering above Crantle, encased in dark green armour like a reptilian shell. The face was hidden behind a helmet that covered the head, eyes shielded by dark shutters that reflected Crantle's own frightened face. Thin, bloodless lips pursed in what might have been contempt. Or amusement.

Crantle's only defence was the wooden staff he held. He brandished it in front of him, waiting to see what the creature would do next, trying to decide if he was safest to stand or to run. He didn't expect it to speak.

'Primitive!' the towering figure rasped, its voice a harsh whisper. 'You will ssssurrender to usss.' It took a lumbering step forwards, reaching out towards Crantle.

He reacted without thinking – slamming the heavy wooden staff into the creature's chest. The creature swayed slightly under the impact. Crantle drew back the staff to strike again. But the creature moved faster than he had anticipated. A clamp-like hand grabbed the staff between the stubby fingers of its gauntlet, ripping it from Crantle's grasp. Then the creature hurled it away, the massive hand now reaching for Crantle instead.

He took a step backwards, turned to run. But too late. The creature's armoured hand closed on the back of Crantle's neck. He felt himself lifted into the air. The world was a sudden blur of confused motion – trees, ice, the creature's impassive face, snowy ground racing towards him. Then darkness.

The Ice Warrior watched the humanoid's inert body for a moment, checking for any signs of continuing life. But there were none. It gave a hiss of satisfaction. Above, the sky was split apart by the blazing path of another ice meteor. A third followed close behind. They impacted one after the other further along the ridge, just inside the treeline.

The Warrior stepped over Crantle's body and made its way towards the nearest of the meteors.

Chapter 2

By the time the Ice Warrior reached the nearer of the two meteors that had crashed down nearby, the Warrior inside was already smashing its way out. It stood in a shattered mass of ice, staring out at the night-clad landscape around it – the snowy ridge that stood between them and the small town of Christmas, the undulating terrain, the darkening woods.

The two Warriors saluted each other with a hiss of satisfaction. So far there was no indication that the Church of the Papal Mainframe had detected their arrival. Inert within the ice, all communications and technology stripped out of their armour, the hope was that there was nothing to detect – no emissions, no processor leakage, no power source.

'Where is Lord Ssardak?' the second Warrior said. 'Did you see him arrive?'

The first Warrior gestured towards the woods. 'His ice capsule came down nearby.'

They set off at once, lumbering through the snow towards the darkness of the wood.

Behind them, a curious figure peered out from behind

a scraggy bush. He brushed his icy hair out of his eyes, and hurried after the Warriors, careful to keep well back and out of sight. When the Warriors disappeared into the trees, he waited for a while, anxious not to make any sound that would give away his presence, then followed.

Immediately, it was dark. The skeletal branches and gnarled trunks of the trees screened out the pale light of the moons. Ahead of him, he could hear the massive creatures forcing their way through the undergrowth and vegetation.

The third meteor had ripped a hole through the canopy of the wood. The huge ball of ice seemed to glow in the moonlight shining down through the gap between the broken trees. A thick mist clung to the ground as the ice slowly steamed and thawed. The two Warriors marched up to the ice, mist swirling round their feet. In unison they raised their huge fists, and together smashed them into the ice.

Watching from nearby cover, the man who had followed them into the wood saw the Warriors tearing away the ice. Finally, they stepped back, and a third figure emerged from the shattered remains of the meteor. Slightly shorter than the Warriors, sleeker in close-fitting armour that was somehow elegant rather than brutal. A dark cloak hung beneath and behind his elongated helmet, and when he spoke his voice was less laboured than the Warriors' rasping tones.

'Essbur, Zontan – you have done well.'

The Warriors saluted their lord, fist to breastplate.

'The components will arrive soon,' Essbur – the first Warrior to arrive – hissed.

'We must observe,' Zontan added.

Lord Ssardak nodded. 'These trees obscure the view. Show me the quickest way out of these woods.'

The Warriors turned and headed laboriously back the way they had come. The man watching them pressed himself back into the undergrowth and held his breath. Only when the Warriors had passed did he let out a relieved stream of steaming air. It choked off as a heavy fist clamped down on his shoulder.

He wasn't a short man, but his head was barely up to the shoulder of the Warrior that heaved him out of his hiding place. The creature's free arm was raised, ready to hammer down. The man braced himself for the impact.

'Wait,' Ssardak ordered. He strode up to the man and looked down at him. 'He may be useful.' Then he turned and continued to follow the other Warrior on his way. The Warrior dragged the man roughly after them.

At the edge of the wood, the four figures paused. Two huge Warriors, the tall, aristocratic Ice Lord, and the dishevelled human in a damp, hapeless coat.

'Who are you?' Lord Ssardak demanded.

The man shrugged. 'I live here, that's all. Saw the fireballs. Came to look. I didn't mean any harm. I wasn't going to interfere. Can I go home now?' he added hopefully.

Ssardak leaned down, so close that the man could see his own thin face reflected in the dark shields over the Ice Lord's eyes. 'I am Lord Ssardak. These are my Warriors – Essbur and Zontan. If you try to escape from us, they will kill you. Do you understand.'

The man nodded furiously. 'What do you want?'

'First, your name.'

'You can call me Elias.'

'You know this area?'

Elias nodded. 'I've lived here a long time. I know it as well as anyone.'

Ssardak gave a hiss of satisfaction. 'Then watch.' He jabbed his fist at the sky – where four tiny points of light were streaking between the stars, growing steadily brighter and larger.

'What are they?' Elias breathed. 'Shooting stars?'

'Ice capsules, like the ones we arrived in. Only much smaller.'

'You mean – there's something inside them? More of your Warriors?'

Ssardak glared at the man. 'I said they were smaller. What is inside does not concern you. Seeing where they come down does. Now, watch.'

They stood in silence as the capsules sped towards them, screeching overhead and disappearing into the distance in a blaze of fire. Sparks and flame shot up from each of the four impact points further down the valley.

'Now tell me,' Ssardak said, turning to Elias, 'and I know that this close to the Truth Field you cannot lie – can you help us find the capsules?'

'Yes,' Elias said. 'But so many meteors in one night – other people will have noticed. They'll be looking too.'

'You mean the Doctor?'

Elias nodded. 'Anything out of the ordinary, and he's right in the middle of it.'

'You know the Doctor?' Essbur hissed.

'Everyone knows the Doctor. Is he why you're here?'

'Why else?' Ssardak snarled.

'Then I'll help you,' Elias said. He sighed and nodded.

Ssardak regarded him closely. 'You would betray your own people?'

'I've done that before,' Elias said. There was a tinge of sadness in his tone.

'Why would you help us?' Zontan demanded.

'Life has changed here since the Doctor came. Before that, if the stories are true, Christmas was a peaceful, happy place. Since the Doctor arrived, I've been scared for my life almost every day.'

'So we can trust you?' Ssardak said.

'I'll help you find your ice capsules,' Elias said.

'That much is evidently true. But will you betray us? Will you tell the Doctor about us, about the capsules?'

Elias smiled thinly. He wiped the snow from his forehead and eyebrows with the back of his hand. 'Like you said, I can't lie, not here. And I promise you, I shan't say a word to the Doctor about you or about what you're doing.'

'Then you will help Essbur and me recover the capsules,' Ssardak said. 'Serve us well, and we shall let you live.'

Elias nodded. 'The nearest of your capsules looked like it came down the Glade of Everdell, just past the frozen brook. I'll take you there.'

He started out across the moonlit landscape, wading through the thick drifts of snow. When he glanced back, he saw that Ssardak and Essbur were close beside him. But the other Warrior, Zontan, had turned and was striding off in the other direction.

'He's going the wrong way,' Elias protested. 'None of your capsules fell back there. Where's he going?'

'It need not concern you,' Ssardak hissed. 'Zontan has

a different mission to complete. But we are all working to the same ends.'

Essbur nodded, reaching out a massive arm and pushing Elias forwards. 'The death of the Doctor.'

Chapter 3

A group of about a dozen people made their way through the snowy fields towards the ridge. Despite the bright moonlight, they carried lanterns. Several of them had shovels. As they reached the top of the ridge, they split into pairs, each heading off in a different direction to continue their search.

'If he's so keen to find these fireballs,' Mattias grumbled, 'why isn't the Doctor with us?'

'He can't be everywhere at once,' his wife Maria pointed out. 'But he's searching too. If he thinks these fireballs are important, then we should look for them. The Doctor will find us soon, you'll see. He'll be with some of the others now, and I bet they're not half as grumpy as you are.'

'I didn't have to come,' Mattias grunted.

Maria linked her arm through his as they walked onward through the snow. 'No, you didn't. But here we are.'

Two hours later, Maria was the one complaining. She was cold and tired, and they had found nothing. 'Perhaps we should just give up and go back home,' she said.

As she spoke, a tall, lanky figure hurried up to them, bounding through the snow with enthusiasm.

'Give up? We can't give up now. We've only just started.' The Doctor turned to look up at the sky, opening his mouth wide to let several snowflakes fall in. He snapped his mouth shut. 'Oh, taste that snow. That's a good harvest of snow, that is.'

'Why are we looking for these fireballs?' Mattias demanded. 'What use are they to us?'

'To us? Nothing at all.'

'Well then.'

'But they must be useful to someone, or else why send them? Tell me that, eh – why send them?'

'All right,' Maria challenged. 'Why?'

'Well, I don't know,' the Doctor admitted. 'But I think we should find out, don't you? Don't answer that,' he added quickly. 'Look, I've told the others we'll meet in the hollow behind Preacher's Clump in an hour, all right? Johann is setting a fire and Old Thom said he'll organise a barbecue breakfast. That's what's so great about the long nights here – you're never far from breakfast. So I'll see you there, yes?'

'Yes, all right,' Mattias agreed. He couldn't help smiling at the Doctor's energetic demeanour.

The Doctor himself was already hurrying off back through the snow, half running, half jumping. 'And if you find a fireball, bring it along,' he called back. 'So long as it's not too hot to handle.'

The best way to recover the ice capsules before anyone else stumbled across them was to split up. Essbur was reluctant to allow the human to go off on his own, but

Ssardak seemed unworried. Later, as Essbur returned with the second of the ice capsules, there was no sign of Elias.

'He will not betray us,' Ssardak assured the Warrior. 'He gave us his word.'

'Is the word of a human to be trusted?'

Ssardak's thin lips twisted into a slight smile. 'Not to trust him would be dishonourable. But he gave us assurances and the Truth Field means he was not lying.'

'What if he does not return?'

'It makes little difference,' Ssardak said. 'But here he is.'

Sure enough, Elias was stumbling back towards them through the snow. He stopped to catch his breath before speaking. 'There are people,' he gasped at last. 'From the town. I think they're searching for your ice capsules too.'

'Did they see you?' Essbur demanded.

'I know how to stay hidden when I want to.'

'Have you located any of the capsules?' Ssardak asked. Elias shook his head. 'You?'

'Two,' Ssardak said. 'They were close together.'

He stepped aside to reveal the capsules lying in the snow behind him. Each was a rough sphere of ice, about the size of the balls the Christmas children kicked around for amusement. Inside its glistening heart, Elias could see the shadowy shape of something frozen inside.

'What is it?' he asked.

'The first components,' Ssardak told him. 'Now we must find the others before the humans stumble across them.'

'One of them came down the other side of that wooded area,' Elias said. 'It's a bit further, but you'll be quicker skirting round the edge than trying to go through.'

'And the fourth?' Essbur hissed.

'Down in the valley, I think. That's where the people I saw were heading.'

'Then we should go there first,' Essbur said.

'They'll see you,' Elias pointed out. 'And I'd be quicker. No disrespect,' he added quickly. 'But if you're hoping to keep this all secret, maybe I should look for that capsule and you get the other one?'

Ssardak reached out and grasped Elias's shoulder as he considered. 'You will tell no one about us, about our presence here,' he snarled. 'Say it.'

'Of course.' Elias's face was twisted with pain. 'I'll tell no one.'

Ssardak loosened his grip. 'That is good. Because if you do, Essbur will kill you.'

'I don't doubt that for a moment,' Elias said, rubbing his shoulder. He forced a smile. 'So, I'll meet you back here, then, shall I?'

Ssardak waited until the human was almost out of sight before giving Essbur his orders: 'Follow him. If the humans have already found the capsule, you will recover it. They will know we are here soon enough – once Zontan completes his mission.'

Further down the slopes, Zontan had almost reached the town. The massive Ice Warrior lumbered through the snow, heading directly towards his target. His mission was simple and straightforward. And once completed would lead inevitably to the death of the Doctor.

*

By the time Maria and Mattias joined the others by the fire, there was a pig roasting on a spit and several local farmers had turned out to see what was going on. There were perhaps twenty people sitting round, warming themselves and enjoying the smell of the imminent breakfast. Maria knew most of them, but not all. Some of the farmers and scavengers out here beyond the ridge kept themselves to themselves.

The Doctor was sitting cross-legged a little way from the fire. In his hands he was turning over what looked like a large ball of ice, juggling it so as not to get too cold. Finally, he set it down on the ground in front of him, and leaned forward to stare intently at it.

'Is that what we've been looking for?' Maria asked as she and Mattias sat down beside him.

'Yes…' he answered absently. Then his face cracked into a wide grin as he looked up at them. 'So you came. Breakfast – can't wait.'

'What is it?' Mattias asked.

'It's a meal you have first thing in the morning. Do you mean to tell me you've never had breakfast before? Oh you are in for such a treat!'

'He means the ice-ball,' Maria explained. 'We know what breakfast is.'

The Doctor nodded. 'Oh yes. Of course you do. If only this was as easy as breakfast.' He picked up the ice-ball again. 'Look – there's something inside, can you see?'

He held it out, so that the flickering flames of the fires shone through the melting ice.

'Why put something inside the ice?' Maria wondered. 'Or did it get caught in a frost?'

'No, this was deliberate. To get it past the technology

scanners.' The Doctor tossed the ball into the air and caught it again. 'It falls past, the contents inert and passive. Just a meteor with some metallic composition. No one gives it a thought.'

'Except you,' Mattias said.

'There are always exceptions. And I *am* exceptional.' He rolled the balls closer to the fire. Its surface glistened and water dripped from it as it started to melt. 'Inside is a component. A part of something.'

'Part of what?' Maria wondered.

'A weapon? Who knows. But they'll want to collect the pieces and put it together. As soon as they use it, our friends upstairs will know, of course.' The Doctor glanced up at the starlit heavens. 'So whatever it is must be pretty devastating. A one-shot shop. Or it does something that won't reveal it as unexpected technology.' He leaned forward to watch the water now running down the side of the ice-ball as it thawed and shrank from the dark shape inside. 'Intriguing, isn't it?'

'But, if it's part of something,' Maria said slowly, 'won't whoever sent it be looking for the pieces?'

The Doctor straightened up. 'Ah,' he said. 'Oh.'

'What?'

'Well, two things really. First, you're right.'

'And second?' prompted Mattias.

'Second – I think they're here.'

He nodded towards the darkness beyond the fire. Maria could just make out a shape approaching – a huge figure, lumbering through the snow towards them.

Chapter 4

'Mattias,' the Doctor said quietly. 'Get everyone back, away from the fire. It's come for the ice-ball. Don't get in its way. Just let it through.'

Several people had seen the creature now. They leaped to their feet. One man – Jedkah – brandished a shovel. 'Who are you? What do you want?' he shouted.

Mattias pulled Jedkah out of the way as the huge creature lashed out at him. Its massive fist caught the end of the shovel, sending it spinning away.

'Back!' Mattias yelled. 'Everyone back, out of its way. Let it get the ice-ball and it'll just go away.'

'What is it?' Maria asked as they all gathered on the far side of the fire.

'Ice Warrior,' the Doctor told her quietly. 'It'll swat you away like a fly if you try to stop it. No sense of humour, though. Not a lot of laughs with the Ice Warriors.'

One of the men was slower than the others getting out of the creature's way. The Warrior shoved him roughly aside. The man cartwheeled away in a flurry of snow and cries of pain.

'Mattias!' the Doctor prompted.

He didn't need telling again. Mattias grabbed the ball of ice from beside the fire and hurled it at the approaching Warrior. It narrowly missed the Warrior's head and landed in the snow nearby.

At the edge of the group, one of the farmers turned and ran – hurrying back to the safety of his home, no doubt. Perhaps he was the sensible one, Maria thought.

Ignoring the people now, the Ice Warrior reached down to retrieve the melting ball of ice, grasping it firmly, then turning and stamping away, back into the night. Immediately several people hurried to help Benedick, the man who had been knocked aside.

'What now?' Mattias asked as the creature was swallowed up by the darkness.

'We need to get back to Christmas,' the Doctor said. 'At least, I do. Why don't you all stay and have breakfast. Make sure Benedick is all right.'

'But – that Ice Warrior creature has what it came for,' Maria said. 'Part of a weapon you said.'

'Yes, but they've got to put it together yet,' the Doctor told her. 'Insert tab "A" into slot "B" and all that. It'll take them ages, and then they'll probably get it all wrong and have to start again. I always do. So we're quite safe.'

'You really think so?'

The Doctor sighed. 'No, not for a moment. We're on the very edge of the Truth Field here, but even so I can't lie to you. This is just the beginning. So like I said – I need to find out what's really going on, and you all need to eat your breakfast.' He stared off into the darkness, the Ice Warrior's footsteps stamped through the snow showing where it had gone. 'I think you're going to need it.'

*

Elias was angry. Essbur and Ssardak watched impassively as he stamped in the snow and waved his arms.

'You could have hurt someone. Actually – you *did* hurt someone. There was no need. I had it all in hand.'

'You were there, with the other humans,' Essbur hissed.

'Of course I was. They know me – I live near here. They weren't surprised when I showed up. I was waiting for a chance to retrieve your precious ice capsule.'

'Was the Doctor present?' Ssardak demanded.

'Of course. He was examining the ice capsule, which is why I couldn't get it. But he put it down, near the fire, to melt while they all ate breakfast. Another few minutes and I could have sneaked it away without them even noticing. Instead your Warrior blundered in and started throwing people about. So if the Doctor didn't know you were here before, he certainly does now.'

For several moments the only sound was the rasping breath of the Ice Warriors. Then Ssardak decided: 'It is unimportant. I have recovered the other capsule, so we have them all. And soon Zontan will complete his mission.'

'So what happens to me?' Elias asked quietly.

'Keep away from the town, and you will survive.'

'You mean, I can go?'

'You have served us well, as you promised. We shall honour our agreement.'

'You're not worried I'll warn anyone?'

Ssardak gave a throaty, coughing laugh. 'It is too late to warn them now. If you are in Christmas when we execute our plan, then you will die with the Doctor and the others.'

'You'll kill innocent people as well as the Doctor?'

Essbur stepped menacingly towards the man. 'Casualties are inevitable. Be thankful that you helped the Ice Warriors. That you know of our plans.'

'Oh, I am,' Elias told him. 'Believe me, I am.'

For a moment, he held the Warrior's impassive gaze, staring into the depths of its shuttered eyes. Then he turned without another word and walked off into the snow.

Stealth was all important until Zontan had completed his mission. Until then, he needed to remain unobserved. The massive Warrior was not used to hiding and avoiding confrontation. If he had been able to bring his sonic disruptor, he could simply have walked in and completed his task. But the Grand Marshal had insisted they could not take the risk of the disruptor being detected. No weapons, no communications – just standard armour, and the inert components that Lord Ssardak and Essbur would now be retrieving and assembling.

So Zontan remained in the shadows, concealed where the night was darkest beside an old barn at the edge of the town of Christmas. His destination was within sight – also right at the edge of town. Massive metal gates across a snow-strewn pathway leading up to the main building. Inside, Zontan knew, was what he sought.

The machinery was automated. But several humans were present to ensure it ran smoothly. Occasionally one would emerge from the warmth of the interior to look at the sky and perhaps make a note of how much snow was swirling through the air. As the night progressed,

Zontan built up a picture of the human schedule – how often they checked outside, how frequently they serviced the machines, when the humans were replaced by other humans...

Finally, at what he calculated to be the optimum time, Zontan emerged from the darkness and marched towards the metal gates. Flickering lamps powered by Christmas's inefficient and unreliable generators cast distorted, broken shadows of the Warrior across the ground.

A thick chain secured the gates, looped through the metal and held by a large padlock. Zontan ignored the chain, and forced the gates open. The chain clanked and protested, shrieked, and snapped – broken links scattering in the snow. As Zontan approached the main building, the snow around him thickened. He could see the flakes swirling upwards from a wide chimney thrust high into the night sky, silhouetted stark against one of the moons. As they swirled up from the snow farm, the flakes were so tightly packed they looked like a thin column of steam.

The heavy wooden doors to the main building opened easily. For a moment Zontan stood on the threshold, checking for any sign of life from inside. All he could hear was the heavy clanking of the turning cogs and gears, the slopping of the water from the spring below the ground gurgling up into the snow-chambers. The compressors that chilled the air to below freezing, and the whirr of the fans that blew the new-formed snow up and out of the chimney to disperse across the landscape ready for harvesting.

It took him a few minutes to find the main control

section. Even the massive Warrior was dwarfed by the ancient machinery as he stood at the simple panel, inspecting the various levers and dials, switches and read-outs. Zontan gave a hiss of quiet satisfaction as he located the controls he needed. A lever pushed to maximum. A wheel clicked forward several notches. A valve opened to its full extent.

Zontan waited as the new settings took effect. The machinery responded sluggishly and inefficiently. But the sound of the huge engines deepened and the noise of the rushing water intensified. Needles swung to the full extent of their dials. The glass snow chambers turned from swirling globes of white flakes to a cloudy mass of congealed snow.

There was just one thing left to do. Zontan gripped the sides of the control panel in his powerful fists, and ripped it away.

With the controls locked at maximum, the thin trail of steam-like flakes from the main chimney became a billowing cloud as the snow blizzarded out across Christmas.

Chapter 5

The Doctor had not been back in the Clock Tower for more than a few minutes when there was a hammering on the door.

'Here for centuries, and not a moment's peace and quiet,' he muttered as he went to answer it. 'All right – I'm coming,' he called out as the hammering increased.

On the wooden step outside was a bedraggled boy in a cap that was too large for his head and pulled down low over his eyes. Snow was piled up on top of the cap. The overall effect was rather comical, but the Doctor knew from experience that it was not tactful to laugh out loud. Instead he allowed himself a smile.

'Symon, isn't it?' the Doctor said. He lifted the boy's cap off his head, shook the snow off and returned it to its cranial position. 'What can I do for you? Broken your Rill puppet again, have you?'

The boy was breathless, presumably from all that hammering on the door. 'It's snowing,' he finally managed to gasp.

The Doctor smiled indulgently. 'It's Christmas. It's always snowing.'

'No, but – it's *really* snowing.'

The Doctor frowned. Symon's cap was almost in need of another emptying. 'The Snow Farm?' He peered past the boy, hoping to make out the distant chimney. But the air was thick with snow and he could barely see across the square.

'I think maybe it's gone wrong. I thought you should know.'

'I think I should,' the Doctor agreed. 'Thank you, Symon. Tell anyone you see that they'd better stay inside until this blizzard is over, will you? That includes you – get home, and stay indoors.'

The boy turned to go. Then he hesitated – one last question: 'Are you staying indoors too, then?'

The Doctor fixed him with a sympathetic look. 'In snow like this? No chance. Handles!' he called, 'mind the shop while I'm gone. If anyone calls, tell them "No".'

He retrieved his coat from a hook on the back of the door, toyed briefly with the notion of a hat, then turned his collar up and headed out into the blizzard. It really was very cold, he thought. And very blizzard. Definitely real snow. Well, snow from the Snow Farm, but rather more of it than was intended. There was a chance – just a chance – that something had gone wrong. But if he was a betting man, then the Doctor would have put good money (if he had any) on the snow being connected to whatever the Ice Warriors were up to.

With this in mind, he headed not for the Snow Farm itself, but for a point between the Snow Farm and the ridge above the town. Visibility was down to just a few metres and he seemed to be spending more time than he'd like blinking snow out of his eyes. But dimly through the whiteout, he finally managed to discern the large lumbering form of an Ice Warrior. Clearly in its element, the creature was wading through the deepening drifts as it made its way up the incline.

The snow was getting heavier. The Doctor guessed that the Warrior had angled the output from the main chimney towards the ridge. But why? He trudged on, his coat thick with snow now. It was in his hair and his eyebrows. His boots seemed about twice the size they had been when he set off. He paused to shake himself suddenly and violently like a large upright dog back from a bracing swim. It wouldn't be long before he'd have to do it again, he knew, but it helped.

Less encrusted, the Doctor pressed on, following the Warrior as it made its way inexorably onwards. He kept well back, but had to judge it carefully. He didn't want to Warrior to see him, but too far away and he'd lose sight of the Warrior. And the creature's footprints offered little help as they filled up almost as soon as they appeared.

The Ice Warrior crested the ridge. It stood for a moment, silhouetted against the snow-strewn moonlight, looking back down into the valley where the town of Christmas lay nestled beneath a thickening white blanket. The Doctor sheltered behind a mount of snow, pressing himself into its cold embrace, listening for any clue that the Warrior had moved on. But all he could hear was the sigh and whisper of the wind.

After a while, he risked peeking over the top of the mound. The Warrior had gone. The Doctor struggled out of the mass of snow and up the final slope. His legs sank in up to his knees, so it was like wading through treacle. Not that he had ever actually waded through treacle, but if he ever did this was surely what it would be like.

At the top, he paused for breath and to wipe his eyes clear of snow. Through the swirling flakes, he could see the Warrior ahead of him. In fact, he could see two Ice Warriors and an Ice Lord – all standing around a collection of metal components. And all staring back at him. He waved.

Getting down the slight incline to join them was easier than struggling up the slope. The Doctor half ran and half tumbled into the scooped-out hollow where the Warriors were waiting. They had chosen an area in the shadow of a clump of moon-pines, so the blizzard was less fierce here. They seemed to be partway through assembling whatever device the various components from the ice capsules made when fitted together. The Doctor took it in at a glance, then – his suspicions confirmed – turned his attention to the Ice Lord. It was best if they didn't think he was at all interested in what they were building.

'Well, isn't this cosy,' the Doctor said, clapping his gloved hands together so that they sprayed a snowy mist. 'I think the weather's taken a turn for the worse.' He nodded at the nearest of the two Warriors. 'I assume that was your doing? Nipped off down to the Snow Farm did you, pumped up the volume?'

'That was my mission,' Zontan hissed.

'Well, jolly good. Well done.' The Doctor clapped his hands together again. 'Keep the snow harvesters in business for a while, I should think. Until we get it fixed.'

'It will not be fixed,' Lord Ssardak told him.

'You think?'

'I know. The town will be destroyed long before the damage can be repaired.'

'I see.' The Doctor nodded sadly. 'To kill one person, you're prepared to destroy a whole town. It's a strange concept of honour you have.'

'You know nothing of honour!' Ssardak snarled. 'We are here to prevent a war that would kill countless billions.'

'You don't need to kill anyone,' the Doctor told him levelly.

'You knew why we were here,' Ssardak said, standing close to the Doctor, staring down at him. 'We warned you to stay away from the town. We have kept honour with you.'

'I suppose you have,' the Doctor agreed quietly.

'So why have you returned, Elias?'

Chapter 6

'I came to warn you,' the Doctor said. 'Amongst other things,' he added, as it was impossible to lie. But he didn't have to elaborate.

'Warn us?' Essbur gave a coughing laugh. 'We fear nothing.'

'Oh, I believe you. But I came to warn you anyway.'

'Warn us what?' Ssardak demanded.

'That the Doctor knows what you are planning.'

'Our plans are too advanced for him to stop us now.'

'Are you sure about that?' The Doctor shrugged. 'Well, you can't lie, so I suppose you must be. But you're wrong.'

'The Doctor knows nothing,' Zontan said. 'How could he?'

'He's not stupid. He knows you've sabotaged the Snow Farm. Only one reason to do that.'

'Which is?' Ssardak said.

'To make snow. Obviously. Lots of snow. Lots and lots and lots of snow, and most of it directed up here to the ridge above the town. Doesn't take a genius, though of course the Doctor is a genius, though I say so myself...'

He frowned. 'Scrub that, forget I said it.'

'The Doctor is not a genius?' Zontan asked, evidently confused.

'No the other bit. He *is* a genius. But look, don't worry about it. I'm just saying that what you're planning is clever, I grant you. But it's pretty obvious. And it's doomed to failure.'

Ssardak took a step closer to the Doctor, regarding him suspiciously. 'There is something different about you, Elias.'

'Everyone's different, that's what makes us who we are.'

'No – different from before. You seem more confident. You seem… angry.'

'Frustrated too,' the Doctor agreed.

'Why?'

'Because before I was just helping you get your bits and pieces together. Now I'm trying to save your lives. And, just for the hell of it, everyone else's lives too. But consider that a bonus if you like.'

'And how can you save our lives?'

'By persuading you to give up and leave. Just go. The Doctor can take you up to the Papal Mainframe's ship in orbit up there.' He pointed at a particular bit of the sky. Then moved his finger to point at a different bit of sky. 'Sorry, I meant up *there*.'

'We have our orders,' Ssardak said. 'The Doctor must die. It is regrettable that others will die too.'

'If you know our plan, you must stay here with us,' Essbur said.

'That decision is so wrong I won't even start to explain why,' the Doctor told him. 'But why don't you finish assembling your sonic cannon and then maybe we can talk about it.'

Ssardak's fist shot out and grabbed the Doctor's shoulder, grasping it painfully tight. 'How do you know what we are constructing?'

'The Doctor guessed from the component he saw in the ice capsule.' The Doctor shook himself free. 'It's clever, I'll give you that. A sonic emission will just seem like the Doctor playing with his sonic screwdriver. No cause for alarm upstairs. Not until it's all over and the Doctor is dead. And even then it'll seem like an accident, won't it. That's why you need all the snow.'

'Our mission is compromised,' Essbur hissed angrily.

'Of course it is,' the Doctor countered. 'That's what I've been trying to tell you. The Doctor knows *everything*.'

Ssardak turned away with a snarl. 'He cannot know everything. He would have evacuated the town.'

'It was too late by the time he worked it out. No one can escape in this blizzard. Not far enough fast enough, anyway. The Doctor,' he repeated, 'knows everything. Everything except the exact frequency of your cannon, but he reckons that to do the job, to shear the snow face, it must be on a setting of, what, about 73.5? Something like that?'

'74.2,' Ssardak replied. His whole body seemed to stiffen slightly as he spoke, as if he was surprised by his own words.

'Yes,' the Doctor said quietly. 'The Truth Field does that sometimes. Catches you unawares. It still gets me now and again which can be very embarrassing, I don't mind telling you.'

He took a step backwards as Ssardak approached. The

snow was piling up and it was difficult to move without falling over. The Ice Lord stood in front of the Doctor, towering over him, snow sprinkled across his helmet, shoulders and breastplate. Behind him the other two Warriors watched impassively. Standing brutal against the undulating white landscape.

'When we first met,' Ssardak said slowly, 'I asked you your name.'

'So you did, Lord Ssardak.'

'You said – your exact words were: "You can call me Elias".'

'I'll take your word for it.' The Doctor grinned to show how unconcerned he was. It was about the only way to lie here.

'But that is not an answer to the question. If you had answered, you would have to tell the truth, but instead you made a statement that did not answer. "You can call me Elias" is not a lie, but it does not reveal your name.'

'It's clever though, you have to admit.' The Doctor backed away, wading awkwardly through the snow. As he reached the edge of the hollow, it was getting deeper – up to his knees. 'It did the trick.'

'A trick?' Essbur echoed, lumbering forwards with surprising speed. Zontan was close behind him.

'What is your name?' Ssardak demanded. 'Tell me, or my Warriors will kill you.'

'And if I do tell you, I think they'll kill me anyway. Though in fact – and this really *is* the truth – saying my name, my actual real name, is the very last thing you want. Really.'

'Who are you?!' Ssardak roared.

The snow swirled round the Doctor's head. It lodged

cold and wet in his mouth as he grinned. 'I thought you'd never ask.' He said. 'I'm the Doctor.'

Even though Ssardak must have been expecting this, the revelation stunned him for a moment. For just long enough for the Doctor to turn and fling himself out of the hollow. He ploughed through the snow, struggling to put distance between himself and his would-be assassins. From behind he could hear a confused hissing and snarling as the Warriors came after him.

For all their clumsy size, they were in their element. The snow slowed them down, but nothing like as much as it encumbered the Doctor. It was an inconvenience to them. It could be the death of him. He struggled onwards, flailing like a drowning swimmer. Sank into the snow so deep the world went first moonlit white and then deathly dark.

Somehow he escaped the cold embrace, flopping over the edge of the ridge, and looking down towards the distant lights of Christmas – all but blotted out by the snow. It looked further away than usual, and the Doctor realised this was because it was. The constant snow had raised the level of the ridge. Tonnes of it falling across the frozen ground. The flakes were so close together now it was like an unbroken white curtain descending across the valley.

He felt himself falling forwards, his centre of gravity over the point of no return – about to tumble into the void. Then he stopped. Pain seared through the Doctor's lower leg as something viciously strong clamped tight about his ankle. Abruptly, he was dragged back through the snow, scrabbling to get a grip and stop the movement. Hands grasping only handfuls of cold wet white.

The grip loosened slightly as the Warrior, he couldn't see which one, reached forward for a better hold on the Doctor. He felt his coat yanked violently, and knew he had only one chance. With a cry of pain and exertion and more than a little anger and hope, he yanked his foot free. In the same movement, he shrugged out of his coat and plunged forwards again.

Cold became freezing. His face was full of snow, biting into his skin and eating through his clothes. A dark blur to his side as the other Warrior charged through the snow, sending up a blizzard of its own. The Warrior behind him lunged forwards again with a snarl of rage.

Then he crested the ridge for the second time. And now nothing held him back. The Doctor's cry changed from hope and pain to fear and surprise as he tumbled forwards, rolling into a ball of ungainly arms and legs that gathered snow and speed as it plunged down the slope.

As he realised that he was free and clear, he opened his mouth to yell a final, defiant cry of 'Geronimo!' But his mouth filled with snow and it became a choking cough of excruciating cold.

On the ridge above, if he had been able to see through the tangle of flailing limbs and the veil of falling snow, the Doctor might have made out three figures standing dark and impassive, silhouetted against a full moon. Proud and defiant.

'He has escaped us,' Zontan rasped.

'There is no escape from the Ice Warriors,' Ssardak declared.

'He is returning to the human settlement,' Essbur said.

Lord Ssardak nodded. There was perhaps just a hint of regret in his voice, just a suggestion that he admired the man who had tricked them. 'Where he will die.'

Chapter 7

'The thing about Ice Warriors is that they're efficient, but not really all that subtle.'

The Doctor's voice was muffled as his head was inside the casing of the main control panel. There was a flash, a smell of singed hair, and a bump as his head connected sharply with the top of the casing.

'Are you all right?' Mattias asked.

The Doctor's head slowly withdrew. As well as the fact he was soaking wet, he now had a black mark down one side of his face.

'I think that's the live one,' he said. 'Which is good. It's terrific. It means I'm nearly there.' He reached his arms into the Snow Farm controls again, pushing most of his upper body after them.

Mattias and the others gathered round watching patiently. Snow was blowing in under the door. Finally, the Doctor's head withdrew again.

'That should do it,' he said brightly.

Everyone turned to look at the snow chambers – which were still whited out. The Doctor frowned, and thumped the side of the damaged console. 'That should do it.'

Sure enough, the globes slowly began to clear. Moments later, the main doors opened and a rather bedraggled Symon ran in.

'It's stopping,' he gasped. 'The snow's stopping.'

'I'll fix this properly later,' the Doctor said, jamming the damaged control panel back on top of the unit. 'Got to fix those Ice Warriors first. Right – everyone in the square outside the Clock Tower in five minutes.'

The air was crisp and cold, but for once the sky was clear. The moons and stars and spaceships cast a combinative luminance across the square where the locals gathered. The snow was over their boots, cladding the buildings in thick white blankets.

'Right,' the Doctor announced, 'Council of War. Or Council of Siege anyway. Perhaps it's an Emergency Committee. But whatever we call it, I thought I'd better warn you all…' He broke off, lips pressed tight together and forehead lined with concentration. 'A warning – that's what it is. Knew I'd get there eventually. Sorry for the confusion. But yes – a warning.'

'What about?' Maria asked.

'Well, about *that* mostly.' The Doctor pointed past the Clock Tower, up at the ridge. 'Snow!'

There was an expectant silence.

The Doctor nodded. 'Yeah, got your attention now, haven't I? Snow. Lots and lots of snow. And a couple of Ice Warriors with their Lord Ssardak who arranged it all. In particular they arranged for it all to fall on the ridge, piling up deep and crisp and even. Well, perhaps not that even. Possibly not very crisp. But certainly deep. Oh yes, I can confirm that "deep" it certainly is.'

'Are they going to build snowmen?' Symon asked. The other children with him giggled and laughed. One of them stuffed a snowball down the back of Symon's neck making him shriek.

'No,' the Doctor said patiently. 'Not snowmen. They are building something, though. It's a sonic cannon.'

'Out of the things that fell in the ice-balls?' Mattias asked.

'Exactly. They've got all the bits and pieces, so we don't have long until they have it assembled.'

'And is a sonic cannon like a sonic screwdriver?' Maria wanted to know.

'Very similar. Same principle. But much more powerful. Which is why they've brought it. OK, so they do use a lot of sonic technology, but if they fire their sonic cannon the emission will just seem like my sonic screwdriver going off, which happens all the time.'

'They're going to shoot at us?' someone asked from the back of the crowd.

'No, actually. That's the clever thing. They need to make it look like an accident or a natural event, so there's no suspicion that the Ice Warriors were involved. Or even here.'

'Make what look like a natural event?' Symon asked, scraping snow off the back of his neck.

The Doctor looked at him like he'd just asked whether adding one and two made three. 'The avalanche,' he said.

It took a while for the Doctor to restore calm and make himself heard. 'Look, don't blame me – I'm just telling you their plan. They have a sonic cannon, set to resonate on a setting of…' He paused to check his sonic screwdriver. 'A setting of 74.2. They'll aim it at the base of the snowfall on the ridge, and shear away that entire section. The whole lot slides down the slope, gathering speed and more snow as it goes. I'm sure they've done the calculations, so by the time it reaches us here there will be tens of tonnes of ice and snow, not to mention any other debris picked up along the way. It will shatter the buildings, bury the town, kill everyone. Simple.'

There was utter silence now.

On the ridge above the town, three dark figures could be seen moving a large, cumbersome object into position. Moonlight glinted on the bare metal of the sonic cannon as the Ice Warriors aimed it down at the snow.

'So,' the Doctor said, looking round at the assembled townsfolk. 'Any questions?'

Chapter 8

Lord Ssardak watched as Zontan calibrated the sonic cannon. Essbur was examining the snow piled on the ridge, working out the exact position and depth to aim the sonic beam. It was a moment that should have been full of pride and accomplishment – the culmination of Ssardak's mission.

But the Doctor's words had unsettled him. Not just the comments about civilian casualties. That was war, and Ssardak was well versed in war. But why had the Doctor returned? Why had he risked his life to warn them, unless he truly believed that their plan was going to fail? He went over the details again in his mind. The best plans were the most simple, and this was elegant in its simplicity. No – nothing could go wrong.

'We are ready to fire, Lord Ssardak,' Zontan reported. 'The point of impact has been calculated. The sonic cannon is set to 74.2.'

'The Doctor knows the frequency we are using,' Essbur pointed out.

'We cannot change it now,' Ssardak told him. 'It has been calculated as the exact frequency necessary to melt a layer of snow of the optimum thickness to provoke an avalanche.'

'He may know the settings,' Zontan said, 'but he can do nothing. This is our element. The snow is our friend.'

'Begin the power-up sequence,' Ssardak ordered. He stepped closer to the brow of the ridge, looking down at the lights in the valley below. He could see people gathered outside the Clock Tower. It would be a quick death for them, at least. 'Prepare to fire.'

The Doctor seemed more preoccupied with adjusting his sonic screwdriver than he did answering all the questions. At last he gave the device a final prod, and looked up.

'Well, obviously there isn't going to be an avalanche,' he said.

A low rumble came from the ridge behind them, rising slowly in volume and pitch.

'They're preparing to fire,' the Doctor explained. 'I did warn them. Now then…' He raised his sonic screwdriver. '72.4 I said, didn't I?'

'No,' Mattias told him. 'You said 74.2.'

'Did I?' The Doctor frowned. 'Are you sure?'

'Yes.'

'I don't think so.'

'Yes, you did,' Symon shouted.

'Perhaps we should take a vote on it.'

'Doctor!' Maria warned. She pointed up at the ridge. 'Whatever you need to do, just do it.'

The Doctor looked too – to see the three Ice Warriors standing beside the sonic cannon. The noise continued to rise and increase.

'Right. 74.2. Although,' he told Mattias, 'if you're wrong and a shed load or more of snow comes down that slope, on your head be it.'

'That seems likely,' Mattias muttered.

The Doctor turned back to face the ridge. He raised his sonic screwdriver, and hoped his calculations were right. The tip of the sonic screwdriver glowed fiercely, and the device emitted a high-pitched whine.

People clapped their hands over their ears as the sound drilled into their heads.

'What are you doing?' Maria gasped.

'Wave enhancement,' the Doctor said over the increasing noise. 'They're using sound waves to melt the snow. If I hit the right frequency, I can enhance the wave they're using.'

'And what will that do?'

'Melt more of the snow faster than they intended. A lot faster.'

'How will that help?'

The Doctor smiled sadly. 'I did warn them,' he said. 'Wait and see.'

'Power-up sequence completed,' Zontan reported. 'The sonic cannon will fire in three… two… one…'

As he spoke, another sound was added to the noise of the cannon. A high-pitched whine emanating from the town below. In the square, Ssardak could see the Doctor, standing on the steps up to the Clock Tower, hand raised in defiance.

Holding something.

His sonic screwdriver.

74.2 – the Doctor knew the sonic setting.

Essbur gave a snarl of anger and realisation at the same moment as Ssardak saw the danger.

'No!' he roared at Zontan.

But too late. The sonic cannon fired into the mass of snow in front of them. Zontan stared at the controls, transfixed and confused by what they told him. Enhanced and amplified by the Doctor's sonic wave, the readings leapt off every scale.

Essbur moved quickly. He lunged for Ssardak, wrapping his arms round his Lord in a desperate effort to protect him. They both knew it was a futile gesture.

The Sonic Beam scythed into the snow – not a directed, focused beam of heat but a huge explosion of massive intensity. The whole ridge disappeared in less than a second – melted, boiled, vaporised in an instant. The entire landscape became a sudden cloud of superheated steam blasting outwards.

The sonic cannon melted in moments.

The last thing Lord Ssardak saw over the glistening, molten shoulder of his Warrior's armour, was a white fog. Then the shields over his eyes ignited in the heat and the steam exploded through his armour boiling the flesh from his body.

The Doctor clicked off his sonic screwdriver and stuffed it into his jacket pocket. A long, low cloud was rising like mist from the top of the ridge. When it cleared, the Ice Warriors and their weapon were gone, along with most of the snow.

For a moment there was silence. Then a scattering of applause. Someone slapped the Doctor on the shoulder. Old Addam was playing a tune on his tin whistle. The applause became clapping in time to the music. People were starting to dance.

'You did it again,' a voice said – maybe it was Mattias. He wasn't really listening.

Yes, he'd done it again. Every life saved was a bonus. Every hour, day, year he bought the town was to be cherished. He watched the mist thinning and dispersing in the cold night air. Every hour, day, year had a cost. There would be tales told, plays acted, embellishments added… But no one would remember Lord Ssardak or Zontan or Essbur. No one except the Doctor. Well, he'd warned them. It was their choice. Quietly, he pushed them gently into a safe place in his memory along with all the others.

Then he grinned, clapped his hands together, and joined in the dancing.

An Apple a Day...
by George Mann

Chapter 1

All across Christmas, the snow lay deep and crisp and even.

Here, on the outskirts of the town, it formed a thick crust across the landscape, undisturbed, pristine. Flurries descended from the heavens like icing sugar being sprinkled upon the world, dusting the rooftops of buildings, smothering the paths.

To Pieter, it barely mattered. He'd never known anything but the snow, and despite the bitter chill, he felt cheerfully optimistic. Harvest festival was approaching. He'd always loved the harvest. Not simply because it represented the culmination of another year's hard work – quite literally, the fruit of his labours – but because of the way in which the townspeople all came together to share in the celebrations.

The festival would last two days, during which the townspeople would erect effigies of the Green Man in the central square, woven painstakingly from strands of ivy. They would dance until their legs gave way; play riotous games with the children and, Pieter's personal highlight, hear stories recited to them by the Doctor.

Every year since Pieter had been a boy, the Doctor had sat upon the steps of the Clock Tower in the dying hours of the festival and regaled them with tales of his adventures amongst the stars. There was something intoxicating about these stories of other, distant worlds, and to Pieter, who had barely left the confines of the town in all his thirty-seven years, they seemed exotic, outlandish and wonderful. Of course, there was no doubt in his mind that they were true – the Truth Field meant that nobody in the town, the Doctor included, could peddle falsehoods. And so the townsfolk would gather, steaming mugs of mulled cider clutched in their hands, to hear the Doctor relate his tales.

Pieter wondered what strange creatures they might hear of this year – more of the Krotons, the Nimon, the Squall, or something new and even more bizarre? He certainly hoped so.

He considered this as he trudged through the snow towards the orchard. It was still early, but it was time to work. If he were lucky, if the Green Man had blessed him this year, his crop would be abundant and ready for harvesting. He would send for the lads from the village to come and help with the picking, and by tomorrow and the start of the festival, the work would be done.

He rounded a bend in the road – now barely discernible because of the snow, but marked by a smouldering brazier – and there, sitting squat on the hillside, was the glass dome of the orchard. It looked like a glowing jewel, nestling amongst the snowdrifts, full of light and warmth. He felt a swell of pride. He'd inherited this patch from his father ten years earlier, and had tended it well, each year delivering a bigger and better yield than the last. This year, he hoped, would prove no exception. If things went according to plan, perhaps he might even be able to afford the repairs he needed to make to the farmhouse.

Pieter clapped his gloved hands together and sighed, his breath fogging in the frigid air. He was looking forward to easing some warmth into his tired bones and resting for a while in his favourite spot, once he'd finished his inspection.

He trudged along the path, his boots kicking up clods of snow. As he drew closer, however, he noticed something had blemished the usually smooth exterior of the glasshouse. Across most of its surface, snowflakes were pattering against the warm glass and immediately beading into water droplets, streaming down the sides of the dome to freeze again around the base. But up on the roof, steam was forming in a lazy spiral, as if it were curling from the spout of a boiling kettle.

Heat was escaping into the chill air. He had a hole. Something had breached the reinforced glass of the dome. If he weren't quick, his entire crop would be ruined. Worse, if the snow got inside, his trees themselves might die of frostbite.

Panicked, Pieter hurriedly stumbled the rest of the way to the dome, fumbled the key from his pocket and opened the door. He stepped inside, pulling the door shut behind him. To his relief it was still warm inside, and his initial fears seemed unfounded. The apples on the trees looked healthy and undamaged by frost. But what could have caused such a hole?

Shedding his hat, coat and gloves and tossing them over a wooden bench by the door, Pieter hurried along an avenue of tall trees, his face upturned as he searched for the breach in the roof.

It wasn't difficult to find. A few hundred metres into the dome it became apparent that something had struck the glass with reasonable force. The hole was about the size of a man's head, jagged and uneven, and thin fractures traced spider webs in the surrounding panes. Eddies of snow danced around the wound, turning to drizzling, pattering rain as the snowflakes passed into the warm interior of the dome.

Pieter felt broken glass crunch beneath his boots, and glanced down. The fragments lay all about him in the mulch, glinting like spilled water in the artificial light. And there, just a few feet away, was what he took to be the culprit – a green, spherical pod, about twice the size of his fist, nestling beside the base of a tree. He approached it cautiously. It looked organic, although it was covered in a thick, scaly hide. The outer skin was cracked and puckered, exposing what he took to be a softer, fleshy interior. It looked like a seed, but if it was, it was unlike any seed he had seen before, and far larger.

How had it fallen through the roof of his orchard? Someone must have thrown it. That was the only explanation. One of the other farmers, envious of Pieter's success and attempting sabotage, or else one of the lads from the town trying to impress his friends.

Well, he wasn't about to let it stop him. He'd dispose of the pod, whatever it was, and fix the hole in his roof. He'd still be ready for the festival, if he set his mind to it. It was frustrating, but he wasn't afraid of a bit of hard work.

Pieter stooped down and scooped up the pod in both

hands. It was heavy and warm to the touch. In fact, now that he was holding it, he could feel it trembling slightly, as if something inside it was stirring. He watched, fascinated, as the fleshy hide began to peel back like the petals of a flower opening in the spring.

For a moment, nothing happened. Pieter realised he was holding his breath, and let it out just as a thick, green vine whipped out from inside the pod and struck the back of his hand.

He cried out in shock and pain, dropping the pod to the ground. He glanced at the back of his hand. He was bleeding. That *thing*, whatever it was, had attacked him! He staggered back, feeling suddenly woozy. Had it poisoned him?

Everything had happened so suddenly, and now he couldn't think straight. His thoughts were like treacle, slow and ponderous. He called out for help, knowing deep down that it was no use – that there was no one nearby to hear him – and then the world suddenly shifted and went black.

Chapter 2

'Doctor! Doctor!' Theol charged out of the alleyway, jumped to avoid an oncoming cart and nearly went head over heels on the ice, slipping and sliding across the street while flailing his arms like a bird attempting to take off. Seconds later he was lying in a heap amongst three empty barrels, with the driver of the cart shaking his fist at him as he trundled by.

Laughing gleefully, Theol scrambled to his feet, dusting powdery snow from his trousers. He leaned on an upturned barrel for a moment, catching his breath.

The central square was a hive of activity, as the whole town, it seemed, involved themselves in preparations for the harvest festival. To his left, Jerl Tompkinson was setting up the big gramophone trumpet with the help of his two boys, and across the square from him, old Jemina Peace was erecting the tent for the puppet show. Around them, others were setting up stalls and trestle tables that, come tomorrow, would be piled high with all manner of sweet delights and celebratory treats. Theol could hardly wait. His mother, he knew, was baking her special syrup and fig buns, and he'd been promised that, if he were good, he could expect an early taste that night before bed.

More interesting than all of that, however, were the group of children about Theol's own age – ten and three quarters – who were slipping and sliding all over the place on a large patch of ice. Theol recognised some of them from school. What were they up to?

Still a little breathless from his run through the streets, and feeling rather hot and uncomfortable under the collar, Theol came out from behind his barrel and stomped through the snow towards the Clock Tower, momentarily forgetting the reason for his hurried trip across town.

It appeared to be a makeshift skating rink. The other children were laughing and squealing with delight as they slid into one another, or swung each other around, or raced from one end of the rink to the other. Theol grinned. Last year, he'd had so much fun skating around on the frozen duck pond with Fral Henderon and the others, before they'd been called away by their parents and told that it wasn't safe. 'If the ice cracked…' his mother had said, wagging her finger, '*then* there'd be trouble. You're to stay off that duck pond, Theol Willoughby, mark my words!'

Dutifully, Theol had done as his mother had asked, and this year, despite Fral's whispered encouragements, when the duck pond had frozen over he'd kept well away. But this! This was different!

He edged towards the rink, drawn towards the fun.

'Hello, Theol!' he heard someone say from close by. He turned to see the Doctor sitting on the steps of the Clock Tower, holding a long rubber tube in one hand.

Beside him, on the step, was the strange robot head that he seemed to carry around everywhere with him.

Theol frowned. 'What's that, Doctor?' he asked.

'Ah, you see, that's what I like about you, Theol. Perpetually *interested*. Inquisitive, even,' said the Doctor, beaming. Theol waited for his question to register. 'Oh, yes!' the Doctor continued a moment later. '*This*.' He waggled the rubber piping. 'This is a hosepipe, Theol, connected to the water supply inside the Clock Tower.'

Theol nodded. 'So *that's* how you made the skating rink,' he said, smiling.

'Precisely!' said the Doctor. 'It's so cold out here that it freezes over in a few moments. Just have to top it up every now and then, and – hurray! A skating rink for the harvest festival.' He looked thoughtful. 'I don't know why I've never thought of it before, really.' He shrugged. 'I suppose it *has* only been a couple of hundred years.'

Theol laughed. He'd always found the Doctor funny. As long as he could remember, the strange man had lived in the Clock Tower at the heart of the town, a sort of wise man, he supposed, who all the townspeople looked to for help and advice. Theol had no idea how old he *actually* was, although the Doctor was clearly older than Theol's mother, with his careworn face, his laughter lines, and numerous flashes of grey in his silly, floppy hair.

'Well?' said the Doctor, expectantly.

'Well what?' asked Theol.

The Doctor sighed theatrically. 'Well aren't you going to give it a go?' He grinned. 'Go on, you know you want to. Get out there and have a slide around. I'd be up there myself if I still had both my legs.'

Theol, however, had remembered the reason for his

trip across town.

'Ah,' said the Doctor. 'You're concerned about your mum, aren't you? Well, don't be. I know she worries about you, but this isn't like the duck pond, and—'

'No, it's not that,' said Theol, interrupting. 'I saw something, over on the other side of town, and you said if I was ever to see anything *interesting*, then I should come and tell you straight away.'

'I did, did I?' said the Doctor. 'I suppose I must have. Sounds like me.' He narrowed his eyes. 'Go on, then, Theol. Tell me something *interesting*.'

'I saw the Green Man!' blurted Theol excitedly. 'This morning, out by the orchard.'

'What were you doing out there?' asked the Doctor.

'Well… I…' muttered Theol.

'Scrumping!' said the Doctor. 'You do know that, *technically*, scrumping's not allowed. And I *am* the sheriff in these parts.'

'I wasn't doing any harm!' protested Theol. 'And besides, I didn't take anything. It's just that I—'

'Hang on a minute!' said the Doctor suddenly, as if Theol's words had only just registered. 'Go back a bit. Rewind. The Green Man, you say? You *saw* him? With your own eyes?'

'Yes!' said Theol, exasperated. 'That's what I'm trying to tell you. He was just there, walking by the edge of the woods.'

'Did he see *you*?'

'I don't think so. I hid behind the bush and watched until he'd disappeared out of sight,' said Theol.

'And what did he look like?'

'He was green!' said Theol, redundantly. 'He had a

ring of leaves and vines around his face. His arms were like knotted branches. It *had* to be him. The Green Man! It's harvest time, and he's come to bestow his grace upon us.'

'Hmmm,' said the Doctor. He was wearing the same expression that Theol's mother would wear when she was convinced he'd been up to no good.

'It's true!' said Theol.

'Oh, I don't doubt it,' said the Doctor, 'but I think you'd better show me, Theol. Could you take me to the precise spot where you saw him?'

Theol looked longingly at the skating rink, and then back at the Doctor. 'Yes, of course,' he said, dejected.

'Don't worry,' said the Doctor. 'We won't be long, and the skating rink will still be here when we get back.' He smiled, and turned away. 'I think you'd better hold the fort here for a while, Handles.'

'Affirmative,' said the strange robot head in reply.

The Doctor put a hand on Theol's shoulder and levered himself up. 'Righto, lead on, Theol! Only, not too fast, eh?'

Chapter 3

Something terrible was happening to him.

Pieter woke to find himself out in the snow, lying face down in a drift. He'd clearly staggered out here in a daze after the plant had stung him, and the cold had brought him round. Only now, he felt somehow… *different*. His limbs were heavy and unresponsive as he tried to push himself up out of the snow, and, more than that, he had the sense that he was no longer alone.

He struggled up onto his knees, glancing around in search of help. Perhaps someone had heard him call out, after all? Perhaps they were here to help.

'Hello?' he shouted, 'I'm over here!' His only response was the empty howling of the wind. 'Is anybody there?' The words felt strangely unfamiliar on his lips. He was desperately hungry. 'Hello?'

There was no one there, just a curtain of tumbling snowflakes, blowing across a leaden sky. A hundred metres away, the sight of the old farmhouse promised warmth, shelter and food. Perhaps that was where he'd been headed, before he'd collapsed here, delirious?

Whatever the case, he had to get out of the cold, and

he had to find something to eat. *Meat.* He had to find meat. Something at the back of his mind was reminding him of that, urging him on. Protein was what he needed, now. Protein would help the pain. He needed to consume flesh.

Pieter staggered to his feet. He felt a throbbing sensation in his left hand and looked down at the site of the sting. He almost recoiled in horror. The flesh around the wound had turned green and scaly, just like the outside of the pod. He tried to prod it with the index finger of his other hand, but that, too, had somehow become gnarled and green.

He tried to fight the rising sense of panic. He'd obviously been infected, and it was spreading. His arm had been almost entirely subsumed by leaves and creeping vines that hadn't just covered his skin, but replaced it entirely. He could feel them now, crawling over his chest beneath his clothes, growing, growing...

Pieter put his hands to his face, and screamed. His hair had transformed into a matted clump of vegetation. Where once he had cultivated a thick, black beard, there was now a mass of rustling leaves. His body was being taken over by the organism from the pod. The vegetation was a part of him, now. It was *replacing* his body, consuming him as it grew.

It was then that Pieter realised that the presence he had sensed earlier was not, in fact, another person from the town who had come looking for him. It was there with him, inside his head. The creature, whatever it was, had wormed its way into his mind. It was whispering to him now, urging him to seek warmth, to find food.

'Get... out... of... my... head!' Pieter whimpered, but

he already knew it was too late. The thing inside him was growing, and the more it flourished, colonising every inch of his body, the weaker he became. He couldn't fight it any longer. It hurt too much.

'Meat,' he said, but his voice had changed, taking on a deep, warbling quality. It was as if someone else – some*thing* else – was speaking through him, and all he could do was watch, like some passive spectator, trapped in the shell of his own body.

'Meat,' he repeated, and took a shambling step towards the farmhouse. 'Trenzalore shall be colonised. All animal life shall become food for the Krynoid.'

Chapter 4

'Blimey, it's cold out,' said the Doctor, rubbing the tops of his arms with his hands as he trudged along the snowy path behind Theol. 'Are we there yet?'

The wind had picked up since Theol's initial outing that morning, and here, away from the shelter of Christmas's buildings, the two of them were very exposed. Icy particles were stinging Theol's face, whipped up from the surrounding fields, and he had to walk with his head bowed in order to see. He wanted to speed up – well, he wanted to be back in the town square, playing on the skating rink with the others – but he was forced to wait for the Doctor, who didn't quite seem able to keep up. He walked with a pronounced limp, dragging his left foot through the snow.

'Doctor?' said Theol.

'Mmmm, hmmm,' said the Doctor, sheltering his eyes with his hands in order to survey the surrounding snowscape.

'Earlier, when we were talking about skating, you said you'd have joined in "if you still had both your legs". What happened?'

The Doctor lowered his hands and looked over at Theol, who had stopped walking for a moment to allow the Doctor to catch up. 'That inquisitive thing again! Good for you, Theol!' The Doctor dragged his leg the last few metres until he was standing beside Theol. They were close to one of the braziers that served as beacons along the road, and the Doctor warmed his hands over it. Theol didn't know how the Doctor could stand being out in just his shirt and coat – he was wrapped in a thick woolly jumper, an overcoat and a hat, and he still felt cold.

'It's a long story,' said the Doctor, finally, 'and not a particularly interesting one. You know the sort of thing: monsters, saving the world, wooden leg. Same as it always is. It all happened a long time ago, at least by human standards.'

'Well, *I'm* interested,' said Theol. He could never understand adults. Why didn't the Doctor just say if he didn't want to talk about it? Theol himself had lost his father to a monster attack years ago, back when he was very small, and *he* didn't mind talking about it.

'I know you are,' said the Doctor, patting him gently on the shoulder. 'But really, there are much more exciting things afoot.' He chuckled. 'Afoot! See what I did there, Theol?'

Theol shook his head, ignoring the Doctor's terrible pun. 'Like the Green Man?'

'Like *that*, just over there,' replied the Doctor, pointing.

Theol followed his gaze. 'That snowy hillock, you mean?' he asked, puzzled. It looked like nothing more than the usual sort of snow dune that blew up during a storm; a mound of fresh snow in the middle of a field.

'That snowy hillock, Theol, looks suspiciously like an impact crater,' said the Doctor.

'An *impact* crater?' echoed Theol. 'As in, something's landed there?'

'See?' said the Doctor. 'Like I said, *much* more exciting. Come on!'

Theol followed the Doctor as they marched across the snowy field towards the hillock. The snow here was deep and, unlike the path, hadn't been cleared for days. Theol found himself sinking up to his knees with every step, and soon the stuff was in his boots, melting between his toes. His socks were sodden, and squelched uncomfortably with every movement. Despite all of this, however, the Doctor seemed to be managing at more or less exactly the same speed as he had before. Theol put it down to a renewed sense of vigour. The Doctor had seemed different ever since he'd spotted the snowy mound. Younger, even. It was almost as if he derived energy from the very idea that something might be wrong.

'What are we going to find in there?' asked Theol. They were getting closer now, and he was starting to feel a little nervous. 'Nothing dangerous, I hope?'

'Well,' said the Doctor. 'I don't think it's likely to be more Martians trapped in ice, if that's what you mean?'

'Um. Martians? Why do you say that?' ventured Theol.

'Oh, they'd make a much bigger crater, for a start,' said the Doctor, as he disappeared over the lip of the hillock.

Theol rushed to catch up, scrambling up the bank of snow in order to see. The crater wasn't as deep as he'd anticipated, and the Doctor – whose clothes were covered in powdery snow as if he'd actually slid down the crater wall on his bottom – was squatting in the shallow depression, sifting through the fresh snow with his fingers.

'Come on in,' said the Doctor, 'the water's freezing.'

Theol decided to follow the Doctor's example, and, pulling the hem of his coat down and folding it underneath him, sat down on the snow and allowed himself to slide to the bottom. He emitted a little, joyous whoop as, gathering speed and unable to stop, he tipped sideways and fell face-first into the snow.

'Oww!' He sat up again, rubbing his arm. He'd banged it against something hard. He felt for it under the snow. There was a large rock buried there, about the size of the Doctor's robot head. He lifted it out, dusting the snow off with his gloves.

'Oh, well done!' said the Doctor. He looked at Theol in stunned silence. 'How did you know where to look?'

'I… I didn't,' said Theol.

The Doctor gave him a sly wink. 'You're good at this, you know. Let's have a look, then.'

Theol passed him the rock.

'Ah,' said the Doctor. 'Right.'

'What? What is it?'

'It's exactly what I hoped it wasn't,' replied the Doctor.

'Very enlightening,' muttered Theol.

The Doctor rubbed at the rock with his sleeve, removing the last deposits of snow. He turned it around so that Theol could see that it wasn't, in fact, a rock at all, but some sort of green pod with a rough, puckered hide. 'It's clever, I'll give them that. No problem getting through the technology barrier for you, was there?' He patted the pod thoughtfully. 'But where's your sibling, eh? That's the real question.'

'You're not making any sense, Doctor,' said Theol. He was beginning to feel decidedly cold and wet.

'This, Theol,' explained the Doctor, 'is a Krynoid seed pod.'

Theol frowned.

'The Krynoid are a race of parasitic invaders. They live only to consume animal life. Their seed pods travel through space for hundreds, sometimes thousands of years, before eventually finding a suitable planet. Once there, they germinate, first infesting and then finally consuming the local fauna. If one of them manages to achieve primary germination, they will spread across a world in a matter of days, destroying all animal life in their wake. They are utterly deadly, and someone has sent them here, to Trenzalore.'

Theol swallowed. 'And that, there, is one of their seed pods?'

'Oh, this one's inert,' said the Doctor, with a shrug. 'They don't do very well in the cold.'

Theol heaved a sigh of relief. 'Well, perhaps Trenzalore's not as suitable as they think. It's pretty cold here all the time.'

'Only, there is a *slight* problem,' continued the Doctor. 'You see, the thing is, they always travel in pairs, and I very much fear that the other one might have had a bit more success.'

'How do you know that?' asked Theol. The hairs on the back of his neck were beginning to prickle, despite the cold.

'That Green Man you saw this morning?' The Doctor was trying to keep his tone nonchalant, but Theol could tell he was worried. 'Yeah, probably a Krynoid.'

'Then you're saying we only have a matter of days to stop it?' asked Theol.

'Well, kind of... perhaps... more like a couple of hours,' replied the Doctor, wincing. He got to his feet. 'So, when I said we were going to make it back for the skating...'

Theol nodded. 'Don't worry, Doctor.' He brushed the snow from his coat and hauled himself up. 'Come on, the orchard is this way.'

Chapter 5

'Oh, look at that!' said the Doctor. 'You humans really are a resourceful bunch. In the midst of all that snow and ice, you build this.' He waved his arms wide to encompass the entirety of the orchard. They were standing at the foot of the hill, looking up at the enormous glass dome. 'Do you realise, Theol, what a feat of engineering this is? To build a climate-controlled glasshouse the size of an entire orchard, on a snowbound hillside, using primitive technology!'

Theol laughed at the Doctor's enthusiasm. 'The apples don't taste half bad, either,' he said.

'I bet they don't!' said the Doctor. 'Come on!'

He charged up the hill as fast as his legs could carry him, spraying Theol with a sudden backwash of snow.

Theol hurtled after him, all thoughts of his squelching boots now forgotten. 'I know a way inside,' he said, as he caught up with the Doctor a moment later. He was standing before the dome's front door, studying it appraisingly. 'Around the far side there's another entrance, and Pieter rarely keeps it locked.'

The Doctor gave him a sidelong glance. Theol

couldn't tell whether it was approval or disapproval he could read in the Doctor's eyes. Perhaps he wasn't supposed to. 'I applaud your resourcefulness, Theol, but it looks as if this time,' he pushed on the door and it swung open on grating hinges, 'Pieter hasn't locked the front door, either.'

Theol frowned. 'That's unlike him, Doctor. He leaves the other one open as it's close to the farmhouse, and he can keep an eye on things.'

Something was clearly amiss, and Theol didn't like it. The Doctor, however, didn't seem particularly put off by this news, and had already ducked through the door. He appeared to be admiring the apple trees beyond. Theol followed him through and closed the door behind him.

Inside, it was warm, but not quite as warm as Theol had expected. Something definitely wasn't quite right. His sense of unease was growing.

'Look at this place!' said the Doctor, laughing. He turned on the spot, taking it all in. Avenue after avenue of mature, majestic trees filled the inside of the dome, ripe apples dangling like Christmas baubles from their leafy branches. Overhead, brilliant electric lights shone down upon the canopy, giving the impression of daylight, despite the perpetual gloaming of the world outside.

Theol had to admit: it was impressive, although some of the lustre had worn off after so many repeat visits to appropriate apples with Fral. He was sure Pieter knew about their scrumping, but the farmer was a kindly sort, and had likely chosen to turn a blind eye to their misdeeds. They never took more than they could eat.

He watched as the Doctor plucked an apple from a nearby branch, rubbed it vigorously on his jacket, and then took a bite. He munched appreciatively, grinning like a loon.

'I thought you said scrumping wasn't allowed?' said Theol.

'Ah, yes. Hmmm. Well, I won't tell if you don't,' replied the Doctor in a conspiratorial whisper. He held his other hand out to Theol, and inexplicably, there was another apple in it, shiny and red. Theol couldn't quite work out through what sleight of hand the Doctor had managed to produce this second apple, but he took it anyway, popping it into his coat pocket.

'It looks as if your friend Pieter is still around here somewhere. Either that, or he left in a bit of a hurry,' said the Doctor, indicating a coat, hat and gloves which had been dumped rather haphazardly across a wooden bench by the door. He tossed the core of his apple into the undergrowth, then cupped his hands around his mouth and bellowed at the top of his lungs: 'Hello?'

The Doctor's voice echoed amongst the treetops, startling a couple of small birds, which burst from their hiding places amongst the leaves and fluttered away towards the other end of the orchard, squawking noisily. Otherwise, there was no response.

'Hello?' called the Doctor a second time.

Once again, there was no reply.

'Well, I suppose that answers that,' said the Doctor.

'Perhaps he's in the farmhouse,' ventured Theol.

'Yes. I'm sure that's it, Theol. In the farmhouse. Right.' The Doctor didn't sound in the least bit convinced. He clapped his hands together, as if readying himself for action. 'Remind me again, where exactly did you see this Green Man?'

Theol sighed. 'Outside. Over by the woods.' He pointed through the panelled glass wall at the foreboding line of trees on the edge of the farm. Their branches looked jagged and lifeless compared to the vibrant, leafy apple trees inside the dome. The Doctor crouched and peered out, narrowing his eyes. Theol found it difficult to make out anything amongst the shadows.

After a moment, the Doctor stood. 'Well, that doesn't look particularly appealing, does it?' he said, with forced jollity. 'Let's just have a quick look around here and—' He stopped mid-sentence as he caught sight of something overhead. 'Ah. Now that's interesting…'

'What's interest—' Theol followed his gaze, suddenly dumbstruck. 'There's a hole in the roof!'

'Yes,' said the Doctor. 'A rather large one.' He looked worried. 'Right. Come along. We'd better take a look.'

They hurried along the avenue of trees, their boots slipping on the soft, muddy loam. A few minutes later, they were standing directly beneath the hole, raindrops pattering on their heads and shoulders as the snowflakes above swirled into the warm air of the dome and turned to drizzle.

'You're worried this is where the second pod landed, aren't you?' asked Theol.

The Doctor looked impressed. He nodded. 'It's warm enough in here for it to germinate.' He kicked some of the fragments of broken glass about with his foot. 'Now, it must have landed somewhere around… *here!*' He ran over to where the branch of an apple tree was hanging broken and limp from the bough. 'The tree must have taken the brunt of the impact.'

Theol looked at where the branch had sheared,

exposing the fresh, fibrous wood beneath. It had almost been wrenched completely from the trunk. Above it, other branches were splintered and broken too, describing the trajectory of the pod as it fell to earth. 'It came down with some force,' he said. 'Perhaps it rebounded in the opposite direction?'

The Doctor didn't answer. He was busy scouring the surrounding mulch, looking for evidence of the pod itself. Theol decided to put his theory to the test. He backed up, widening the search. If the pod had rolled...

He'd taken no more than two steps before he saw it, a few feet behind where the Doctor was searching. He crossed to the base of another tree and stood over it for a moment, watching it nervously. It looked similar to the other pod they had found in the snow, but this one had flowered open in a star-like pattern, exposing a hollow, fleshy interior. It looked as if it might have disgorged something.

Theol looked up at the damaged apple tree, then back at the pod, mentally working out the angles. It certainly didn't look like the pod had rolled here on its own after landing. 'Umm, Doctor...'

'Shhh!' said the Doctor. 'Concentrating.'

Theol gave him a moment. He considered picking up the pod and taking it to the Doctor, but decided against it.

A minute later, the Doctor appeared at his side. 'Oh,' he said. He sounded a little dejected. 'So, you found it, then. Why didn't you tell me?'

Theol sighed. He didn't think it was worth pointing out that he'd tried.

The Doctor dropped to his haunches, squatting in

front of the open pod. 'This isn't good,' he said. 'In fact, I'd say it was decidedly bad. Most definitely bad. We need to find your friend, Pieter.'

'Because the pod is open?' asked Theol.

'Because the pod is open,' confirmed the Doctor.

'Meaning…?'

'Meaning that someone has already been infected. Meaning that the Green Man you saw was almost definitely the Krynoid, and meaning we really do have to stop it soon before it starts scattering seed pods across the rest of the planet.'

'Oh,' said Theol, unsure what else there was to say. He understood the implication of what the Doctor had said: Pieter was probably the one who'd been infected.

Theol felt something brush against his cheek, and raised his hand to knock it aside. It was a tree branch, probably just blowing in the wind.

He paused for a moment. *The wind.* They were in a giant glasshouse. There *was* no wind. He sensed a shadow creeping over him, blotting out the electric light from above.

Slowly, Theol turned his head. He tried to swallow, but his mouth was dry. One of the trees was *leaning over.* As he watched, one of its branches shifted in his direction, its long, spindly fingers caressing the top of his arm. He heard a creak of rending wood right behind him, and realised, with horror, that more of them were on the move. Leaves rustled as they crept closer.

'Doctor!' said Theol, in a panicked whisper. 'The trees, they're moving!'

'Ah, yes.' The Doctor sounded a little sheepish. 'I might have forgotten to mention that bit.' He slowly began to rise to his feet, pulling Theol up beside him. 'When a Krynoid reaches a certain point in its germination, it manifests the ability to control other plant life in the same vicinity. That means, Theol, there's both good and bad news.'

Theol ducked to avoid a low-swinging branch, aimed at his head.

'The good news is: the Krynoid is obviously still nearby,' the Doctor went on.

'And the bad news?' gasped Theol, thinking he could probably anticipate what the bad news was.

'The bad news is that this orchard has suddenly developed very dishonourable intentions toward us. Run!'

Theol didn't have to be told twice. He ducked out beneath the boughs of the nearest russet, tripping and rolling onto the dirt path between the two rows of trees. He scrambled to his feet as the Doctor came charging out behind him, scattering leaves and bellowing 'Ruuuunnnnnnnn!'

Behind them, the trees had already begun to close ranks, leaning across the path to block their way to the door, and the Doctor and Theol did a quick double-take as they realised there was no chance of escape the way they had come in.

'Just my luck,' said the Doctor, between gulping breaths. 'Trapped in a sealed dome with an orchard full of trees that want to eat me. Clearly it's karma for all those apples I've enjoyed over the years.'

'They want to *eat* us!' cried Theol, fighting a rising tide of panic.

'Well, now we're getting into semantics,' said the

Doctor. 'Still, I don't think we should stick around to find out. You mentioned another door?'

Theol took a deep breath. 'This way,' he said, grabbing the Doctor's sleeve and pulling him in the opposite direction. 'It's just up ahead. Past those, um, trees...'

Chapter 6

'Phew!' The Doctor sank to his knees in the snow. 'That was invigorating. Nothing like a good chase. Love a good chase, me. Gets the hearts pumping.'

Theol was bent double, his hands on his knees, attempting to catch his breath. Behind them, the apple trees were raising a cacophony as their branches chattered at the glass panes of the dome, still trying to claw at them, even now.

It had proved a rather hairy race to the other side of the orchard, with Theol practically dragging the Doctor while they fought their way through grasping branches and pummelling apples, as the trees had suddenly begun to bombard them with fruit in an effort to slow them down. Theol guessed he'd have a few bruises in the morning. Assuming, of course, that he was still alive. He'd already vowed more than once that his scrumping days were over.

Thankfully, as Theol had anticipated, Pieter had left the side door open, and now both Theol and the Doctor were in the snowy yard on the far side of the dome, in the shadow of the old farmhouse. It was a relief to be safely out of the reach of the homicidal trees, at least for a while. He was just about to say as much to the Doctor, when he heard the tinkling of broken glass behind him. He decided not to look back. After all, it wasn't as if trees could *walk*…

The Doctor was getting to his feet.

'What now?' asked Theol.

'Now we find Pieter,' said the Doctor. 'My guess is he'll have gone looking for food.'

'He keeps a larder in the farmhouse,' said Theol. 'The building's a bit ramshackle and rundown, and he doesn't live up here any more, but I know he keeps provisions on hand.'

'Right-i-o! To the farmhouse, then!' said the Doctor, tugging on the lapels of his coat. He was grinning again. Theol decided he was enjoying himself a just a little *too* much.

The entrance to the farmhouse was around the side of the building, and so, cautiously, trying their best to tiptoe through the snow, they rounded the corner and hurried to the door. It was still snowing, and thick flakes seemed to appear out of nowhere, bursting against Theol's hot cheeks. Visibility was poor, and the paltry light of the moon was near enough obscured by the snowfall. His boots crunched with every step.

The door to the farmhouse was hanging open, and a small drift of snow had formed inside the porch. There were no footsteps or impressions in it. If Pieter *was* inside, he hadn't come out again recently. But why would he leave the door hanging wide open to the elements?

'Follow me,' said the Doctor, stepping gingerly over the threshold.

Theol had no intention of doing otherwise, so he simply shrugged and did as the Doctor suggested.

Inside, the farmhouse was cold and dark. There was a sense of abandonment about the place, as if the building hadn't seen proper use for months. In the hallway, the wallpaper was peeling in the damp, a box of old junk had been dumped on the stairs, and the door to the kitchen was swinging back and forth on a single, broken hinge. The decoration and furnishings were sparse at best. Perhaps Pieter had just let the place go, now that he'd moved down to the town with his family?

'Through there,' whispered Theol, indicating the way to the kitchen.

The Doctor nodded and crept across the hallway. He'd produced a slim metal cylinder from somewhere when Theol wasn't looking, which he clutched in his right hand as if it were a talisman. He put his head around the doorframe and peered into the other room. He remained like that for a moment, not moving a muscle, not saying a word. Then, visibly relaxing, he turned back to Theol. When he spoke, it was no longer in a sepulchral whisper. 'When you said the place was a bit rundown, I don't suppose you were referring to a whopping great hole in the wall?'

'No,' said Theol, perplexed. 'Just that the roof isn't quite watertight and it's difficult to heat.'

'Ah,' said the Doctor. 'I suspect it'll be even more difficult to heat now. And probably a little less watertight, too.'

Theol crossed the hall and pushed passed the Doctor, stepping into the kitchen. He saw immediately what the Doctor was referring to – the far wall now contained an enormous, ragged hole, as if something had simply bulldozed its way through the brickwork. Snow was gusting in, scattering across the tiled floor. The fireplace was cold and dead, a dresser had been overturned, and the remains of various foodstuffs had been strewn haphazardly about the room.

'Raw meat,' said the Doctor from behind him. 'On the table.'

Theol stepped aside to let the Doctor pass. He circled the battered old table, grimacing as he examined what looked like a veritable butcher's shop worth of animal remains. Theol wrinkled his nose in disgust when he recognised a raw chicken carcass that had been largely stripped of its flesh. There were teeth marks in the skin. He glanced at the Doctor, a question in his eyes.

'This is what the Krynoid do, Theol,' said the Doctor, waving his metal cylinder to underline his words. 'They consume. They'll devour anything that's not vegetation, anything with flesh and blood and bones. That's why we've got to stop it, before it can seed more of its kind, and before it can grow any stronger.'

Theol nodded. 'Well,' he said, pointing at the hole in the wall. 'I'm guessing it went that way.'

Chapter 7

The Krynoid should have been almost impossible to miss, but at first Theol's brain failed to register it.

He stepped out through the gaping hole in the kitchen wall, carefully avoiding the scattered bricks and fragments of broken crockery. They'd emerged into the large courtyard on the other side of the house; a rectangular service yard bordered on three sides by enormous cattle pens and storage barns where Pieter preserved his apples in the months following the harvest.

Theol glanced around, seeing nothing untoward. He stamped his feet to stave off the cold. Beside him, however, he sensed the Doctor hesitate. 'Um, Theol, if you wanted to go back inside now, I certainly wouldn't think any less of you.' There was an edge to the Doctor's voice, a note of warning that sent a shiver down Theol's spine.

He frowned. 'Why? What's the matter?'

There was a loud, dull thud a few feet in front of them, and Theol looked down to see the half-chewed carcass of a cow, splayed in the snow. Steam rose from inside its torn belly, and crimson blood was spattered all around it, stark and bright against the pure white snow. He felt bile rise in his gullet. How could half a cow simply fall out of the sky?

Slowly he raised his head, looking up at the green thing perched upon the top of the cow pen.

It was almost the size of the farmhouse, a shambling behemoth of vines and vegetation. Theol hardly knew what to make of it. It had no obvious shape or form, other than the writhing mass of tentacles with which it was nonchalantly plucking cows from the pens below. As he watched, the creature lifted a Friesian into the air, smothered the beast with its ropey limbs, and then tossed it aside a few seconds later when it had finished stripping the flesh from the bones. The body landed close to the other carcass, scattering snow over Theol's boots.

'That's… that's…'

'Yes,' said the Doctor. 'That's the Krynoid.'

'Pieter?' finished Theol. 'That's Pieter?' His voice wavered slightly as he formed the question.

'I'm afraid so,' said the Doctor, his voice level. 'Or at least, it was. I doubt very much whether there's much of Pieter left.' He clicked his fingers, suddenly animated. 'But it's worth a try!'

'What do you mean?'

The Doctor cupped his hands around his mouth, just as he had in the orchard. 'Oi! Krynoid, over here!' He waved his hands above his head as he tried to get the creature's attention.

'Doctor!' said Theol, sharply. Was he mad? 'What are you doing?'

'Seeing how much of Pieter's still in there. If he's

strong enough, he might be able to fight it.' He continued to wave his arms above his head like a frantic, gangly puppet.

The Krynoid paused, shifting its bulk to regard them. Theol couldn't see anything that resembled an eye, but it was obvious it knew they were there.

'That's right!' bellowed the Doctor. 'I'm talking to *you*. I want to speak to Pieter.'

The Krynoid made a sound like a windstorm blowing through a metal grate. 'There is no Pieter. The human no longer exists. There is only Krynoid. Soon, there shall be nothing *but* Krynoid.' Its voice was a deep, rasping burr, utterly inhuman. Theol felt the sound reverberate in his belly.

'Come on, Pieter! I know you're in there. Fight it, man!'

The Krynoid allowed another cow to slip from its grasp. It crashed noisily into the pen below. Then, with surprising grace, the creature twisted itself around, sliding down the side of the building and bringing chunks of masonry and roofing tiles with it. It was coming for them.

Theol took a step back. 'Pieter!'

The Krynoid seemed to hesitate for a moment, as if Theol's voice had affected it in some way. 'Pieter?' he said again, quieter this time.

'Theol?' The Krynoid's voice wavered and cracked.

'Yes, Pieter! It's Theol!' shouted the Doctor. 'That's right, fight it. Fight the Krynoid inside. You can do it!'

'I… I… I can't,' said the thing that had once been Pieter. 'I can't hold it off any longer. Theol… run!'

The Krynoid lurched suddenly in their direction,

its vines bristling. It had an odd ambulatory technique that involved propelling itself across the ground with its tentacles, but neither Theol nor the Doctor wished to hang around very long to watch.

'Go around the house!' shouted the Doctor. 'Don't get trapped inside.'

Theol set off at a sprint. The Doctor appeared to consider for a moment, before lurching off in the opposite direction. Theol supposed he was trying to draw the Krynoid off, or at least make sure that one of them made it safely away.

Theol cleared the yard a moment later, stumbling in the snow. He hesitated. The Doctor hadn't come around the other side of the building yet, so he wasn't sure which way to run. He could hear the horrible shuffling of the Krynoid close behind him, and knew he only had seconds to make a decision.

He took off again, heading for the cover of the woods. At least the Krynoid wouldn't be able to get its bulk through the trees. He only hoped the Doctor would be able to keep up.

The wind drove snow into his face as he ran, causing his eyes to stream. He could feel the tears freezing on his eyelids as he blinked them away, and his breath was coming in ragged, choking gasps. He was determined to get away, to help the Doctor defeat this monster. He had to. He had to prove that his dad's sacrifice had been worth it, all those many years ago.

Just as he reached the border of the woods, he heard the Doctor calling to him, and spun around to see what was happening. The Doctor was a short way behind him, waving his arms wildly, and behind *him* the

Krynoid lurched along with alarming speed, its tentacles writhing as they lashed at the Doctor's heels.

Theol backed into the trees, waving for the Doctor to hurry up and join him. 'In here!' he shouted.

'No, Theol!' came the Doctor's urgent reply, almost lost on the wind. 'Not the trees!'

But it was too late. Theol realised his mistake just as one of the trees reached down and wrapped its gnarly branches around his legs.

Chapter 8

'Get it off me!' Theol felt the branches constrict around his thighs, so tight that he thought they might cut off his blood supply. Further branches were beginning to claw at him, tentatively curling around his chest, his arms, his throat.

He closed his eyes, waiting for the pain, waiting for the tree to slowly throttle the life out of him. He didn't want to die. He wasn't *ready* to die!

He struggled, attempting to pull himself free, but the tree only responded by tightening its grip, so hard now that he was beginning to feel light-headed. Stars danced before his eyes like glittering snowflakes on the breeze.

He was going to become food for the Krynoid. Would his mother eventually find his body, abandoned in the snow like one of those poor cows? Or would the Krynoid defeat them all, consume all human life on Trenzalore, and no one would ever know what had become of him, how he'd tried to help the Doctor? He gasped for breath, forcing the chill air down into his lungs.

'Theeeeoooolllll!' The Doctor's voice echoed in his ears, but it seemed so distant, like a half-remembered dream. Theol peeled opened his eyes to see the Doctor charging towards him, propelling himself frantically on his wooden leg, the Krynoid looming large over his shoulder.

'I'm sorry…' he tried to say, but all that came out was a strangled whisper.

And then the Doctor was diving straight at him, leaping through the air like a man half his age and yelling 'Geronimoooo!' at the top of his lungs.

Theol braced himself as the Doctor slammed into him, shoulder first, knocking him backwards and somehow loosening the grip of the branches that held his legs. He fell backwards under the momentum, hearing a sharp *crack* as the wooden limbs snapped under their combined weight, and suddenly he was free, rolling in the frozen undergrowth, all wind knocked out of him. He clutched his belly, trying to force air into his lungs.

'On… your… feet,' gasped the Doctor, righting himself.

Theol scrambled up beside the Doctor. The world gave a sudden, spinning revolution, and then he was breathing again, and the sound of the raging Krynoid filled his ears.

Above them, the trees were shaking violently, loosing a deluge of snow. As Theol watched, they folded back on themselves, parting like a wave to reveal the looming Krynoid. He'd been wrong about using the trees as cover, in more ways than one.

The Krynoid emitted a wet, gurgling roar and lunged at them, striking out with its tentacles. Theol dived to the ground to avoid it, but the Krynoid was not about to give up easily, and, wrapping its appendages around the trunks of the nearby trees, hoisted itself up and into the woods.

Theol was back on his feet and running before he realised what was happening. He was heading deeper into the woods, but the trees were simply parting around him so the Krynoid could pursue. He glanced back over his shoulder to see the Doctor falling behind. 'Come *on*, Doctor!'

'I'll remind you, young man,' huffed the Doctor between breathless gasps, 'that I'm nearly fifteen hundred years old. At least, I *think* that's about right. Could be a few hundred years either way, really.' He flapped his hands dramatically. 'And anyway, whatever my age, running with only one good leg isn't as easy as it looks!'

'*Doctor!*'

The Krynoid roared again, lashing out at the Doctor but succeeding only in upending another tree and showering itself in snow. It seemed to pause for a moment, as if stunned by the sudden, icy flurry.

'That way!' The Doctor suddenly took a sharp right, ducking amongst the trees, and Theol followed suit, barrelling after him. A moment later, he burst out of the cover of the woods to find the Doctor waiting for him on the hillside. Behind them, the Krynoid was still charging through the trees in pursuit, making a fearsome racket.

'It's the cold,' said the Doctor, 'slowing it down.' He put a hand on Theol's shoulder as he caught his breath. 'Did you see what happened when it accidentally covered itself in snow?'

Theol nodded. 'It seemed to be stunned for a moment.'

'Precisely,' said the Doctor, flashing his brightest

smile. 'Just like the other pod, inert in the snow drift. Which gives me an idea.'

Theol was too tired and too scared to be able to feel any sense of relief, regardless of the Doctor's sudden confidence. The rustling in the trees was growing closer by the second. The Krynoid would be on them again at any moment. 'So, tell me,' he said, 'what's the plan?'

'We need to lure it to the town,' said the Doctor.

'The town!' said Theol. 'That's a terrible plan!'

The Doctor shook his head. 'It's a great plan! We need to get it as close to the Clock Tower as possible.'

'And what'll happen at the Clock Tower?' asked Theol.

The Doctor shrugged. 'Either we'll destroy the Krynoid, or the Krynoid will destroy the town.'

Theol sighed. 'Those sound like fair odds,' he conceded.

Chapter 9

Theol had never done so much running in one day.

In fact, he was sure that even if he totalled up *all* the running he'd *ever* done in his life, it still wouldn't add up to the amount of running he'd done today.

His lungs burned, his legs were leaden, and he was having the time of his life. He had no idea how the Doctor was managing to hobble along at such speed on his wooden leg.

The two of them, Theol and the Doctor, came haring down the road into town, slipping and sliding on the impacted snow and whooping with fear and excitement and adrenalin. Hard on their heels, the Krynoid propelled itself across the frigid earth, only a matter of minutes behind them.

'Look out!' cried the Doctor. 'Monsters on the loose!'

Townspeople scattered as they burst into the square, running in every conceivable direction, ducking behind braziers, bushes and benches for cover.

'Whoops! Coming through!' called the Doctor, accidentally overturning a cart with a flailing arm and sending empty barrels careening across the road. The driver bellowed a savoury curse in their wake. Theol didn't have time to look back to see what the driver made of the Krynoid in hot pursuit.

'Here we are,' called the Doctor, skidding to a halt by the steps to the Clock Tower and dropping to one knee as he steadied himself. 'Home sweet home.' He stuck out both hands and caught Theol as he almost went flying by, unable to slow himself on the ice.

Behind them, the Krynoid roared in frustration as they took the steps two at a time, the Doctor pausing only long enough to scoop up Handles – who'd continued his vigil on the steps for the best part of the day – and to whip the strange metal cylinder from his jacket pocket. He pressed a button on the device as they charged towards the doors, and Theol heard the lock mechanism click open. The Doctor grabbed him and bundled him through, kicking the door shut behind them. He activated his cylinder again and the locks snapped shut.

'What is that thing?' said Theol, picking himself up off the floor and dusting himself down.

'This?' asked the Doctor, tossing the device up in the air so that it twinkled in the dim light. He caught it again, slipping it back into his pocket. 'Just a screwdriver.' He crossed the room and placed Handles down gently on a small, cluttered coffee table.

Theol took a moment to glance around. He'd never been allowed inside the Clock Tower before. It was a musty old place, full of accumulated junk and dust. It seemed somehow homely, though, as if the Doctor had made it his own, doing the best with what he had; a hodgepodge of mismatched furniture, a scattering of books, wooden toys, maps, and unfamiliar bits of technology.

All but one of the walls were covered – littered, in fact – with children's drawings, each of them depicting the Doctor engaged in battles against a variety of foes. Theol didn't recognise most of them, but they came in all manner of shapes and sizes. Scrawled notes of thanks accompanied almost all of the pictures. Some of them were now so old the paper had grown yellow and brittle. The Doctor really had been the sheriff here for a long time.

The one wall that hadn't been plastered over with drawings had another distinguishing feature all its own – a large, glowing crack that looked to Theol like nothing so much as a crooked, taunting smile. Bright, pure light seemed to seep from the crack, as if it were a bleeding wound in the very fabric of the building. He was just about to ask the Doctor to explain, when the entire tower shuddered, and he remembered the Krynoid, and the work that was still to be done.

'What now, Doctor?' he said.

'Up those stairs,' replied the Doctor. 'We've got to get to the very top, as quickly as we can. Right up to the bell itself.'

Theol nodded. He could hear the Krynoid probing at the door, its proboscis scratching at the lock. He hoped the Doctor had a *real* plan. One that might actually work.

He rushed up the steps behind the Doctor, his heart thumping. Is this what had happened to his father all those years ago? Is this how it had ended for him, under siege and fighting for his life? Theol's mother had always refused to tell him the story, and all he'd been able to glean from the other children was what they'd heard from their own parents – that Theol's dad had died during an attack on the town. He wondered if the creatures responsible were depicted in some of the pictures on the Doctor's walls, if perhaps the children whose parent's *hadn't* been killed during the attack had written to him in thanks.

Theol paused on the stairway, suddenly stricken with fear. 'You will stop them, won't you, Doctor?' he said. 'It's just, my dad, he died in an attack like this and…' He trailed off, unable to continue.

'I know,' said the Doctor, quietly. 'He was a good man, Theol. The best. And I promise you we're going to beat it. Together.' He reached out and took Theol's hand in his own. 'Come on. We're nearly there. We can do this.'

Hand in hand, the Doctor and Theol climbed the last few steps to the top of the tower.

They emerged into the dark, snowy afternoon. The cold was like a slap to the face, and the gusting wind threatened to lift Theol from his feet. Worse than that, the Krynoid had latched on to the tower and was dragging itself up the side of the building, worming its tentacles into the brickwork, hauling on the window frames. It was utterly relentless. Plasterwork crumbled and dropped to the ground as it heaved itself closer.

'Now, Krynoid, it's time to listen to me!' said the Doctor, raising his voice above the howling wind. He seemed to grow in stature suddenly, his expression hardening. 'You made one big mistake landing on this planet. *One* mistake. You forgot that this planet is protected. Not by me. Oh, no. I'm just a little old Time Lord with a wooden leg, well past his best. No, what you missed, what you *never even considered*, were the people of Christmas. The people down there, in that town square, who are about to show you what they're made of.' He paused, staring at the Krynoid as if willing it to come closer. 'That's today's lesson, big guy. No matter how tall you grow, you should never forget the little people!'

The Krynoid roared, lashing out at the Doctor and wrenching a hunk of the balustrade free, close to where he was standing. The Doctor staggered, but kept his balance. The broken masonry crashed noisily to the ground. In a few minutes, the creature would be at the top of the tower, and within reach of them both.

Theol grabbed anxiously at the handrail, desperately needing something to hold on to while he waited to see what the Doctor would do next.

'Right, you lot!' shouted the Doctor, leaning over the remains of the balustrade and calling to the people below. 'Come on out. Nothing to be frightened of here.'

As Theol watched, some of the townsfolk began to emerge tentatively from their hiding places. They looked terrified. He knew how they felt.

'That's it!' said the Doctor. 'Brilliant! Let's show this monster what Christmas is all about!' He glanced at Theol, a huge grin on his face. 'Snowballs! I want to see lots of snowballs. Chuck them at this big green plant-y thing over here. As many as you can.'

For a moment nothing happened. Then, as Theol watched, a perfect snowball arced through the air, dashing against the side of the Krynoid. It was followed by another, and then another, and then suddenly there was a barrage of them as the townspeople found their confidence and rallied to help the Doctor.

DOCTOR WHO

The Krynoid roared in defiance, but Theol could tell that the sudden, frozen assault was already beginning to slow it down.

'That's it, Fral Henderon. More like that! Keep it up, all of you.'

Theol could hear Fral hooting down below as he sent snowball after snowball hurtling at the Krynoid. Fral had always been good in a snowball fight. He rarely missed his mark.

'Right, Jerl Tompkinson, you're up next,' called the Doctor, pointing at the man whom Theol had seen setting up the gramophone earlier that day. 'See that length of rubber hose down there?'

Jerl's reply was lost in the wind and the defiant screeching of the Krynoid, but he seemed to understand what the Doctor wanted of him.

'That's the one! Right, turn it on, and give this Krynoid a right old soaking.' The Doctor was strutting around on the bell tower, directing things below like some sort of manic conductor, standing before an orchestra.

A sudden spray of icy water shot up over the parapet, showering Theol and causing him to cry out in surprise. He ducked away as Jerl attempted to get the hosepipe under control.

'Steady on!' called the Doctor. 'The monster's over here!'

The jet of water arced through the air, splashing across the Krynoid's hide. It thrashed wildly, but Jerl kept the water flowing, twitching the nozzle from side to side until the whole creature was sodden and dripping.

Theol reached up to wipe a stray droplet from his cheek, but it fell away at his touch, already frozen in place like a tiny, silver tear. It was then that he realised what the Doctor was up to. Of course! The skating rink!

The Krynoid had begun to slow. Its proboscises were barely moving now and it was having difficulty clinging on. Theol could see tiny, sparkling crystals of ice beginning to form all over its hide.

There was a sound like the creaking of old wood, like the ice on the duck pond flexing beneath his weight, threatening to give way. One of the Krynoid's tentacles flailed weakly, and then stiffened in mid air, glistening with ice. The whole creature shuddered, and for a heart-stopping minute Theol thought it was going to rally, but then it was utterly still, like a grotesque statue, frozen in place.

No one moved for a moment, as if everyone in the town were collectively holding their breaths.

As usual, the Doctor was first to break the silence. 'Your turn, Theol,' he said. 'Pass me that rope.'

It was heaped in the far corner of the Clock Tower, coiled like any icy serpent. Theol ran over to it, hefting it with a grunt. It was heavier than it looked. He carried it over to where the Doctor had begun fiddling with the bell pull.

'What are you *doing*?' he asked, as the Doctor tied the end of the rope to the pull.

'Giving the people of Christmas a harvest festival to remember,' he said. He crossed to the edge of the tower and heaved the coiled rope over the side. It unwound as it fell, thudding across the steps below. 'OK, you lot. Give that rope a good heave! Ring the bell for Christmas! Ring the bell to tell the monsters they're not welcome any more!'

Four, six, ten of the people below took up the other end of the rope, bracing themselves as if preparing for a tug-of-war. The Doctor turned to Theol. 'Cover your ears!' he shouted. His own hands were already splayed around the sides of his head.

Below, the townspeople gave a sharp tug on the rope, and the bell swung wildly in its cradle. The sound was almost deafening, and the vibration caused Theol to stagger unsteadily. He dropped to his knees, clamping his palms over his ears. Had the Doctor finally lost it?

He looked up to see the Doctor grinning at him like a loon. Theol frowned, and the Doctor stepped to one side so that Theol could see. Over the Doctor's shoulder the Krynoid shuddered again, but this time it was due to the reverberation of the bell, and as Theol watched, cracks began to form like fault lines across its massive, frozen body.

The people below heaved on the rope again, and this time the Krynoid exploded like so much shattering glass, showering the square in fragments of icy wood and vine. Theol scrambled to his feet, running to the parapet. Below, he could see that the people were cheering, and despite the fact that he couldn't hear anything but the thunderous ringing of the bell, he added his voice to their choir.

It was over. The Doctor had done it. *He* had done it.

Christmas was safe.

Chapter 10

The harvest festival was in full swing when Theol finally emerged from his mother's house the following day. He'd worked most of the night on his gift for the Doctor, and then slept in past lunchtime, woken only by a growling belly and the distant strains of song and laughter drifting in through his window. After discovering his mother had already left, he'd hastily dressed, wolfed down a slice of bread and cheese, and then ducked out into the chill afternoon.

Now, he was weaving through the press of people in the town square, clutching a long, thin package under his coat.

His body ached like it had never ached before – the result of the previous day's exertions, of so much *running* – but nevertheless he felt jubilant. He still couldn't quite believe the adventure he'd had with the Doctor, the part he'd played in saving the town from the Krynoid invasion.

All around him the townsfolk were making merry, swilling tankards of mulled cider and sampling the delights of the myriad stalls. The rich aromas of spiced bread, hog roast and sticky buns reminded him he hadn't eaten a proper meal in some time, and he almost gave in and allowed his belly to lead him off in the wrong direction. He fought the urge – he could wait just a little longer. There was something he needed to do.

A bonfire roared in the middle of the square, hastily erected that morning from the remains of the Krynoid. It was a fitting end, Theol decided – a funeral pyre for Pieter, who had held his ground against the monster when it mattered, and done all he could to save Theol and the Doctor. He'd be sorely missed.

By the Clock Tower, Fral and the others had returned to their makeshift skating rink, squealing and jostling as they tried to outdo each other, attempting to remain upright on the glassy ice and leaping about forming elaborate shapes with their bodies. Theol laughed. He would enjoy joining in with their games in a little while.

The Doctor was sitting in his usual spot on the steps, talking to his robot head. He looked older, somehow. Maybe it was the way the shadows from the bonfire picked out the thin lines on his face, or just the way he was sitting, hunched over, as if all the energy had seeped out of him. Theol wandered over and picked a spot next to him. He set his package down on the step beside him.

'This is nice, isn't it, Handles?' said the Doctor. He was staring out at the bonfire, at the people milling around, chattering and laughing and dancing.

'Nice is irrelevant,' replied the head in its grating monotone.

The Doctor smiled. 'Well, everyone else seems to be having a good time.'

'Affirmative.'

The Doctor sighed. 'You know, a long time ago, I used to know a dog who had just about the same level of conversational skills as you. I wonder what he's up to now.'

'Information not available,' replied Handles.

'Not, I didn't think so,' said the Doctor. He glanced round suddenly, as if noticing Theol for the first time. 'Hello, Theol. How's your mum?'

Theol laughed. 'Furious. I was supposed to help her with the syrup and fig buns. I completely forgot.'

The Doctor smiled. 'It's only because she's scared, you know. She doesn't want to lose you. That's why she worries so much.'

'I know,' said Theol. 'Maybe now she'll trust a little more that I can look after myself.'

'I wouldn't count on it,' said the Doctor, grinning. 'Mums are mums, after all.'

Theol laughed. 'I'm glad we were able to save mine,' he said. He could see her now, busily handing out her buns from a stall on the other side of the square. She looked happy. 'I'm glad we were able to save them all.'

'So am I,' said the Doctor.

'I was thinking,' said Theol, 'what about the other pod? The one we found in the snow?'

'In there,' replied the Doctor, nodding in the direction of the bonfire. 'Better to be safe than sorry.'

'So that's it, then?' asked Theol. He tried not to sound too disappointed. 'It's all over.'

'For now. Until the next time. Until another arrogant race or faction or fan club attempts to find a way through the barrier. But I'll be here, Theol. I'll be waiting.'

They were silent for a moment, both staring into the

dancing flames of the fire.

'Oh, I've got something for you,' said Theol, reaching into his coat pocket and fishing out an apple. He tossed it to the Doctor, who caught it in his left hand.

'An apple a day…' he said, laughing. He took a big bite out of it, nodding appreciatively.

'There's this, too,' said Theol, grabbing the long, thin parcel from the step and passing it over.

The Doctor accepted it with a curious frown. 'What's this?'

'Open it!' said Theol. 'Go on!'

The Doctor set about unwrapping the present, peeling off layers of multicoloured paper. 'You've wrapped this well,' he said, waggling his thumb to try to shake off a piece of errant sticky tape. 'It reminds me of Chri—' He stopped suddenly, extracting a gnarled wooden stick from the remnants of wrapping paper. It had a smooth, curved handle and a cork stopper on the other end. The Doctor turned it over in his hands, running his fingers along its polished surface.

'It's a walking stick,' said Theol. 'I whittled it last night, from a fragment of Krynoid. I thought we had to save something of Pieter, something useful to remember him by.' He swallowed. 'I hope it's all right.'

For a minute the Doctor looked as if he were about to say something, but then changed his mind. He was quiet for a moment. Then, sighing, he put a hand on Theol's shoulder. 'Humans,' he said, quietly. 'You never cease to amaze me.' He waved the stick in the air before him, as if he were a champion fencer weighing up a new sabre. 'It's perfect,' he said. 'Absolutely perfect. Thank you, Theol.'

'It's to help you run a bit faster, next time the monsters

come.' Theol beamed. 'So you can try to keep up with me.'

The Doctor grinned. 'You know, your father would have been very proud of you, Theol. He was there, the day I lost my leg. He was very brave, too. Just like you.'

Theol looked up at him, wide-eyed. 'He was there? You were with him when it happened?'

The Doctor smiled, but there was a hint of sadness in his eyes.

'Let's hear a story, Doctor!'

'Come on, give us a tale.'

Theol looked up to see a crowd was gathering around the bottom of the steps. They were all watching the Doctor with expectant, excited expressions.

Theol started to get to his feet, feeling that the time was right for him to slip away, but the Doctor caught his arm. 'Stay,' he said, quietly, and Theol returned to his place on the step.

'All right, all right. Settle down, you lot!' said the Doctor, cheerily waving his arms for quiet. He looked round at Theol, and winked. 'Today I'm going to tell you the story of how I lost my leg...'

Strangers in the Outland
by Paul Finch

Chapter 1

After so many years prospecting in the wilder zones of the Outland, Tiberius and Yalala were used to the extreme cold. But in the depths of winter, the air temperature could drop even lower, the frequent blizzards exacerbating this with a terrifying wind-chill.

Tiberius often considered that he ought to take his daughter back into Christmas, at least until spring arrived – though this was never a high priority. In forty years spent scouring the Outland, he hadn't yet found the mother lode, which made him all the more determined to keep trying. He knew there were precious metals out here because he'd found placer fragments in alluvial deposits where ancient creeks had once run, so as a rule he didn't take the time to retreat from even the most bitter winter winds. And if 8-year-old Yalala ever complained about it – which she rarely did, to her immense credit – his stock response was to swathe her even deeper in furs and woollens. Ultimately of course, despite her tender years, Yalala was too useful a pair of hands to dispense with even temporarily. She was already strong enough to wield an ice-pick and a shovel, and he'd taught her how to pack and place a boronite charge.

Not that having so young and willing an assistant meant life out here was any the less a tale of unrelenting hardship.

Tiberius often pictured them as a pair of pathfinders from the old colonial days of the Americas – he'd never visited Earth of course, but he'd seen pictures in history books. One big difference was the near-perpetual night of Trenzalore; that had never been a problem for those ancient American pioneers, and they'd often enjoyed the advantage of having horses or mules to carry both themselves and their equipment. Tiberius and Yalala benefited from no such beasts of burden – only Howzi and Mowki, their indefatigable snow-dogs, though neither looked especially canine when gambolling across the snow in their trousers, tunics and special dog-shaped balaclavas, which Tiberius had fashioned for them out of two handsomely patterned rugs.

It was Howzi and Mowki who first saw the objects falling from the sky.

They were drawing the sled slowly along Devil's Elbows Canyon, a Z-shaped passage bisecting the frozen rocky ridge called Fafnir's Crest, and opening just south of the vast moon-pine forest known as the Tundra-Vald. They had emerged from the Choke, the canyon's narrowest point, when the dogs slowed to a halt, hot breath pluming from the ends of their colourfully mittened snouts, their saucer-shaped eyes unblinking.

'Mush there, boys! Mush!' Tiberius called, snapping the reins.

The dogs were at first too distracted to comply, and

now he followed their gaze, peering up at the black silk sky, where, very fleetingly, six curious objects trailed down past the silver face of Soror, the slightly smaller of Trenzalore's twin moons.

'And what might this be?' he murmured.

He spoke to himself, but Yalala, sharp-eared as always, heard him. She scrambled up to her knees amid the blankets and mufflers at the rear of the sled, and caught a fleeting glimpse of the last descending silhouette before it vanished from sight.

There'd been six of them in total, Tiberius thought. Curious things; of no recognisable shape. But by their direction and the angle of their descent, they were coming down over the Tundra-Vald. He yanked his scarf aside to scratch at his straggly grey beard; a common habit when he was agitated.

One other reason for keeping his daughter in the Outland was the danger that seemed to lurk around the town. For all its choirs and bonfires, its mulled wine and merry meetings, Christmas was only safe to visit fleetingly and sporadically these days. It didn't matter how highly its occupants thought of the oddball toy-mender in the Clock Tower, or how successful he'd supposedly been in warding off these unexplainable and yet uncountable menaces from the stars – at some point the chap was going to fail. Though his tenancy here had already outlasted Tiberius's entire life, the Doctor – as he was called – was withering with age and stress; he'd already lost his left leg in some conflict or other. By contrast, the Outland, for all its wild beasts and frigid perils, was a safer place in so many ways – and yet now there was *this* mystery.

Christmas was over forty miles south of here, beyond a trackless wilderness. Despite this, logic suggested these new objects from the sky must be connected with all those others occasionally falling – and yet Tiberius's instincts told him differently, and he trusted his instincts implicitly (even if they had led him from crag to plain to ice-filled cave, and on no occasion had rewarded him with more than a few sparkling trinkets).

'Mush!' he shouted again, snapping the reins.

The snow-dogs pressed on, easing up to a gallop. Standing five feet tall at the shoulder, and running seven feet nose to tail, they were a breed specific to Trenzalore and vastly sturdier than any of their cousins on Earth, while their heavy double-coats enabled them to resist the worst ravages of the very worst winters. As such, a mile or so further on, before the sled had even left the Devil's Elbows, the deadfall ended and a fresh blizzard struck, intense blasts of snowflakes blotting out the clumps of moon-pine and the towering, wind-carved rocks, but the team drove gamely on.

They were even more exposed on the plain beyond the canyon, where a fierce westerly was blowing. Yalala buried herself under more blankets and quilts. Tiberius hunched forward over the handlebars, plastered head to toe with white. But this was the kind of endurance they'd been required to show throughout their self-imposed exile in the Outland, and in just under an hour they'd reached the outskirts of the Tundra-Vald, where the westerly slackened into another deadfall – the name given on Trenzalore to the brief lulls between storms – and though flakes the size of goose feathers still fluttered around them, the sword edge of the chill had dulled.

They drove across several outer clearings, where flawless drifts of snow climbed to half the height of the pines.

'Whoa there, whoaaa!'

Howzi and Mowki slowed to a thankful halt, sagging in their woollens.

Tiberius gazed uncomprehendingly upward, to where strips of cloth dangled through the boughs on his right. Daring to remove his rawhide glove, he felt at the nearest piece – it was soft, pliable. Silk, he thought. Briefly, he was excited. He could barter silk in Christmas when he next visited. The most he was usually able to trade in town were furs – hence he did a little trapping and hunting alongside his normal activities. It just about kept him in supplies, but silk was a rare commodity on this planet and would be worth considerably more. It might enable him to acquire some new boronite.

Then, sensing a presence, he glanced left.

Nothing stirred beyond the level, moon-lit surface of the clearing. The nearest trees were shadowy stanchions; the further clumps a silent labyrinth of night-black evergreen.

'Yalala,' he grunted. 'Stay.'

Her pale face peeked through a rent in the bundle of blankets, while he attached the snow-shoes to his fur-wrapped feet, and plodded away.

Yalala always obeyed. Firstly, because she'd known no other course than to follow her father's curt instructions. Secondly, because she knew it was vital if she wished to survive. This frigid realm forbade life to all but the cleverest and most robust. The population of Christmas only ventured out here when necessary, and in small, hand-chosen groups. Even then, they'd sometimes fail to return, having lost themselves in blizzards, sunk into drifts, or fallen down hidden gullies. On occasion, she and her father had stumbled across their pathetic remains – usually encased in ice, with frost-wounds more terrible than anything she'd seen in her worst nightmares.

If she didn't wish to suffer the same fate, it was crucial she follow her father's rules. But soon, after nearly two hours, there was still no sign of him. The blizzard had now ceased completely, and there was a magical stillness, the moon sparkling on the deep, crisp white, and shafting through the black lattice of the pines.

Howzi and Mowki lay alongside her, burrowed partway under the surface, virtually wrapped around each other. They regarded her curiously when she finally stood up in the back of the sled, and paused to listen. Again, nothing moved. The only sound was the distant hiss of wind on the ice-caps. She thought to call to her father, but every part of her body was wrapped aside from her eyes – she didn't even wish to take the muffler from her mouth, as her lips would dry and crackle with indecent speed.

At length, she fitted on her own snow-shoes and stepped out. The very least she could expect now was that her father would scold her. But other fears were more prominent.

What if he'd hurt himself? What if he'd got stuck?

She'd ventured no more than five metres when the dogs began to whine and growl. At the same time, there was lurching movement on her right. She spun around, and her eyes almost popped from their sockets as a great slab of solidly packed snow tilted slowly upright to face her – finally reaching a height of maybe two metres. Even as she stared at it, portions fell away, revealing the basic outline of a man; a torso, limbs and a head, though these too were so caked they were almost indistinguishable. Only as it lumbered forward, its ever-heavier tread crunching the frozen surface, did the final vestiges of snow trickle off, enabling her to see the face beneath.

Yalala still didn't bother to pull down her muffler. Though it remained firmly in place, her terrified shrieks could be heard far across the wintry waste.

Chapter 2

'Strangers in the Outland?' the Doctor said as he slowly descended the Clock Tower stair, his artificial limb creaking and clumping. 'What exactly does she mean by that?'

'It's been difficult getting anything coherent out of her,' Caleb replied from below. He was a rangy young fellow with a lean face and a mop of reddish straw-like hair, only its fringes visible around the edges of his woolly hat. 'Becca says she's in deep shock… The trouble is she muttered a few things that didn't make much sense, and then stopped talking. Be good if you can speak to her.'

'Who is she?'

'Her name's Yalala Gluck. We don't know her very well, to be honest. Her father's Tiberius Gluck. A bit of a recluse – he moved to the Outland after his wife died. Always searching for gold and silver. We occasionally see him. Tends to bring us furs, amber and the like, which he exchanges for food and clothing.'

'A trapper?' the Doctor said, looking boyishly pleased. 'How quaint.'

'You *have* met him before.'

'Have I?' The Doctor wound a scarf around his neck. 'Raccoon cap? Dead shot with a musket? No, wait… That was Davy Crockett. Or was it Daniel Boone? Sorry…' He shrugged. 'No memory of it. You live all these centuries, and start forgetting things that happened a matter of heartbeats ago.'

'It was more like five or six years.'

'That's what I said.' The Doctor turned to his workbench. 'What do you think, Handles? Strangers in the Outland. What's your take on that?'

The battered old cybernetic head sparked to life. 'There is insufficient data to make a proper analysis of these so-called Strangers. The Outland is a subarctic environment, able to support only the hardiest forms of boreal plant-life, which consequently—'

'Yes, yes,' the Doctor snapped. 'We know all that!'

'No inferior native bipedal life forms of any description are registered in the Trenzalore fauna catalogue. However, the catalogue may be expanded if additional discoveries are —'

'No, thank you!' The Doctor shrugged into his overlarge fur coat. 'We're not in the business of exploring Trenzalore. We can leave that to the Tiberius Glucks of this world. What are you standing around for, Caleb? There's no time for dawdling.'

'Sorry, Doctor.'

'My stick, if you please.'

Caleb handed over the Doctor's elaborately carved cane.

'How many strangers did this mysterious child see?'

Caleb pondered. 'She thinks four or five.'

'And how many did her father see?'

'That's just it. He didn't return with her.'

'Ah-ha…' The Doctor's face screwed into a frown as he headed outside, his fur coat so large that it trailed behind him. 'Now that's something I *can* get my teeth into. Takes a flippant attitude to his child-rearing responsibilities, does he? I shall certainly be having a word in *his* ear, tough old coot of an Indian fighter or not.'

He stopped short outside the Clock Tower, where a row of five husky young men awaited him; all bearded and weather-beaten, their colourful village garb only accentuating their burly physiques.

'And what's this?' The Doctor paraded past them sergeant-major style. 'Yoshua… Rubin… Josef… Jerema… Luca…?' He raised a querying eyebrow at Caleb. 'All members of the Lifeboat crew, unless I'm mistaken. Are we going sailing?'

'We thought it might be necessary,' Caleb said.

'Anything for an adventure, eh?' The Doctor struck out across the snowy street to the Moot-Hall. The Lifeboat crew tagged along behind.

'You don't think so?' Caleb asked.

'I think that neglectful parenting was a sad but regular occurrence on Earth,' the Doctor replied. 'And that it was only a matter of time before it followed Man out into the stars. Gluck lives in the Outland – he thinks he can get away with anything, you see.'

'But what about the strangers?'

'How do we know they're strangers to Tiberius Gluck?'

'The girl fled forty miles to get away from them. They can hardly be friends.'

The Doctor swung around on the point of his stick, eyebrows knitted together. 'Forty miles?'

'She had two snow-dogs in harness. Lesser beasts would never have made it.'

'*Forty* miles, Caleb?'

'She came all the way from the Tundra-Vald through the Devil's Elbows. We estimate forty miles at least.'

The Doctor pondered this as he strode on into the Moot-Hall, which was as crowded as usual, though less jovial by far. The ranks of villagers parted as he came through. In the centre, a young girl wearing rough homespun clothing was seated on a stool, her hands bound in fresh bandages, each finger individually wrapped. Nurse Becca, the town's most skilled medical practitioner, knelt alongside her, gentling massaging a diminutive pair of bare, white feet in a bowl of lukewarm water. Despite this, the child shivered, her cherubic features wan even in the rosy firelight. Her lips were thin and pearl-grey; her moist eyes twinkled, though they stared, apparently, at nothing. Her fair hair hung in damp, stringy ringlets.

'Mild hypothermia and first-degree frostbite,' Becca replied to the Doctor's initial enquiry. 'Aside from that, she's in surprisingly good health.'

'Maybe Tiberius Gluck wasn't so negligent a parent after all.' The Doctor chewed the side of his mouth. 'Poor Tiberius…'

'What do you think happened to him, Doctor?' someone asked.

'Excuse me if I don't reply to that question in front of the child.'

'She's too traumatised to even know where she is,'

Becca said, passing a hand in front of her patient's glazed eyes, drawing no response.

The Doctor still said nothing, and they all understood his reticence. The Truth Field was a painfully revelatory aspect of life in Christmas. If, for example, the Doctor suspected Tiberius Gluck had been murdered, and that his 8-year-old daughter was extremely fortunate to have escaped with her own life – such as that life now would be, given what she'd probably seen in the Outland – and he voiced this suspicion aloud, it would not help the morale of the community's more nervous members.

Felix, for one – Caleb's youngest brother – was standing close by, listening with awe. And then there was the child herself.

The Doctor knelt to face her. 'You say her name's Yalala?'

'We believe so,' Becca said. 'Tiberius was very private when it came to family affairs.'

'Yalala?' the Doctor asked gently.

She peered straight through him.

'There's no need to be frightened. You're quite safe now. But you've come a long way on your own. Do you want to tell us why?'

Gradually, as if it required great effort, the little brow furrowed.

'Who were these strangers, Yalala?' the Doctor wondered. 'What did they look like?'

Only after a torturous minute did she actually seem to see him, her eyes slowly refocusing. Her crinkled grey lips puckered into a perfect 'O'. Tremulously, she pointed a bandaged finger at him – and screamed.

Shrilly, intensely, protractedly. Until Nurse Becca and

several other mothers of the community moved in to calm her. But all that time, she screamed, and pointed over their shoulders at the Doctor, who at last shuffled outside into the snow.

Caleb and the rest of the Lifeboat crew accompanied him, bemused.

The Doctor wasn't just their headman, their reeve, their adviser on all things; he was their saviour. If they didn't exactly adore him, because he was inclined to occasional terseness and impatience these days, their respect for him ran deep as the permafrost.

'Doctor?' Caleb finally ventured. 'What does this mean?'

'I'd have thought it was perfectly obvious,' the Doctor replied sharply. 'Whoever Yalala saw out there – or *whatever* she saw – he, or it, looked just like me.'

Chapter 3

The Trenzalore Lifeboat had existed long before the Doctor had taken residence in Christmas. So arduous were the conditions in the Outland that it wasn't launched from its barn-like boatshed any more than was strictly necessary, but it more than sufficed for the job because it was a particularly well-built vessel.

Rather like a miniature version of one of those old-fashioned sailing brigs on Earth, the Lifeboat was sixty feet from prow to stern, yet with an upper deck, two square-rigged masts, and a jib and flying jib at the front, all hung with sails, of course, which its crew would manipulate constantly by ascending the mass of rigging strung between them like spider-webs. The hold in its belly was spacious enough to store any amount of timber and brushwood, not to mention furs and animal carcasses – the gathering of which was the normal purpose of the Lifeboat, though it also came out in times of emergency. In addition, the hold doubled as a cabin for the crew, who needed regular warmth and shelter on long-haul trips. Of course, the Lifeboat wasn't a lifeboat in the Earth sense of the term. There was no surface water on Trenzalore that wasn't permanently deep-frozen – the nearest substantial body of water to Christmas was Lake Lagda, perhaps fifty square miles across and buried under ice. But that scarcely mattered, as the boat sat on a spring-loaded undercarriage with special, giant-sized skis affixed, so when the blizzards caught the vessel's sails, they would drive it at terrific speed across the snowfields.

As always, it required two teams of six snow-dogs each to tow the Lifeboat from the town and eastward along the Vale of Halva, the only entrance into the sheltered heart of the Halva Fells, the circular mountain range in the midst of which Christmas nestled, and along which the sun would shimmer during those few moments it rose above the horizon in summer. The dog-teams were harnessed to port and starboard rather than at the front, for as the fells flattened out on either side, the cyclical winds of the open plain would fill the vessel's sails. The harnesses would then be loosened, and the teams would peel away in safety while the Lifeboat sped on through the storm.

From there on, it was all down to the helmsman.

'We're in the teeth of a northerly,' Caleb shouted to the rest of the crew as he stood on the raised bridge, both hands locked on the wheel, only his eyes visible above his woven scarf. 'Starboard tack to port tack!'

The crew nodded, and went scrambling up the pitch-coated rat-lines to adjust the sails accordingly. Only when the wind changed direction, which it did regularly in the Outland – but predictably, which was why Caleb had a wind-chart covered in glass mounted on his right – could they retreat through the hatches to the hold, where a canteen of hot coffee bubbled on the coal-fired stove.

The Doctor, meanwhile, stood lost in thought at the prow, ignoring the snowflakes whipping past him like arrowheads, though lately even the Doctor had taken to dressing for the cold; donning a woollen cap, scarf and gloves, and of course his immense fur coat. True, he didn't 'over-package' himself the way so many trekking to the Outland did – even now he wore the fur coat open at the front, so that it swirled in the gale – but time was when he'd almost been oblivious to the Trenzalore freeze.

'Doctor, you'll catch your death!' Caleb called, spinning the wheel and commencing the slow curve windward.

The Doctor didn't seem to hear. He regarded the whiteness blurring by in silence, as they breasted the snows with a steady *swiiish* and a regular flap and *thud* of ropes and sails. The lateral resistance of the frozen surface enabled them to maintain a constant, steady course, but at thirty knots it was hardly a smooth ride. The craft jolted frequently, veering and swaying as the streams of wind wove into and around it. Now and then, the ice-shattered stumps of moon-pines loomed past like tortured, wind-twisted spectres. There were other obstacles too: dips and hummocks, towering rock forms, but Caleb knew his job. They bypassed each and every one without a flutter, a trail of billowing powder at their rear.

'Remarkable place, Trenzalore,' the Doctor eventually said, hobbling back along the gritted decking. 'Takes with one hand, gives with the other.'

'I don't understand,' Caleb shouted.

'Well… one doesn't need to understand everything to know it's there. The law of yin and yang, negative and positive, dark and light.' The Doctor glanced out across the moonlit emptiness. 'Everything's unusually well-balanced here.'

'Well-balanced… We barely see daylight.'

'That's just the point.' The Doctor dug Caleb's shoulder with a gloved finger. 'There's almost no sunlight, so what does Nature do? It gives you two moons, Soror and Frater, which creates lunar-synthesis, allowing plant and animal life to flourish. Look at these temperatures…' He scraped a layer of frost from the front of the thermometer glass. 'By any standards of human history, they'd barely be survivable… yet your ancestors found a snug little alcove in the mountains. Not only that; you've got all these nice flat surfaces – and a constantly shifting tide of wind to propel you smoothly across them.' The Lifeboat jolted as it hit some hidden obstruction. 'Well, almost smoothly. I suppose a ride with no bumps would be a bit boring. The point is you can live here, you can travel, you've got everything you need. And yet it's hardly an attractive place, so no one's likely to come and try to…' His words tailed off.

'Take it from us?' Caleb suggested. 'I suppose that's the other thing, isn't it?'

The Doctor pulled a mournful face. 'Yes it is, rather.'

'That's the other bit of balance. No one in their right mind would ever want to live here. Yet all kinds of enemies are massing out there somewhere… or so you tell us.'

The Doctor patted his arm. 'It's not the ones out

there we've got to worry about, Caleb, it's the ones down here… the strangers.'

Caleb spun the wheel to bring the craft about. 'Any thoughts on who they are yet?'

'A fairly obvious one, actually.' The Doctor looked dejected again. 'But it's not pleasant. I'm afraid your spears and crossbows won't be much use.'

As well as loading the hold with their survival packs, their skis, snow-shoes, horns and the like, the Lifeboat crew had also brought a few weapons. Most of these had been adapted from farm-tools, but ultimately amounted to little more than toys, none of them properly designed for combat. The aforementioned crossbows, of which there were only two, were next to useless in this situation: small, lightweight items designed and made mainly for hunting purposes.

'The strangers will be in the same boat, won't they?' Caleb said, sounding mildly concerned.

'Hopefully not in the *same* boat, Caleb.' The Doctor dug his arm again with an air of forced bonhomie. 'As in *this* boat. That would never do.'

'You know what I mean… with regard to weapons.'

'Yes… I mean, theoretically. Though they'll still have a kind of advantage.'

'Well, we ought to know soon enough. Look what's ahead.'

The lengthy escarpment that was Fafnir's Crest bisected the extremity of their vision; a slow ascending wall of ice-covered rocks and rubble, its upper ridge a hard white line on the purple snow-cloud, stretching in either direction as far as the eye could see. No one, not even the Doctor, knew if it was possible to skirt around it – they'd never been that far – so usually they had to go through it. Far to the east was the Goat Path, a zigzagging foot-trail leading right the way over the top, though only the hardy or foolish ever attempted that. The main route to the other side was the Devil's Elbows. From this distance, it was no more than a v-shaped bite in the escarpment, a tiny dent – but up close it would be colossal, more like the Cumberland Gap, that ancient mountain pass in the Appalachian Mountains of North America through which those early explorers had followed the famous Wilderness Road.

Almost unconsciously, the Doctor hummed a ditty. 'Da-vee… Da-vee Crockett, king of the wild frontier…' He sighed. 'Poor Tiberius.' Though, of course, if what he feared they now faced was actually real, it might be more a case of 'Poor Christmas'.

Chapter 4

An hour later, the wind direction changed, as per Caleb's chart, enabling them to tack towards the Devil's Elbows at greater pace.

As they traversed the S-bended canyon, those crewmembers not needed on deck came up anyway, to watch in wonder as the sloped mountain walls soared up to either side, their snowy flanks broken only by shadowy blots of moon-pine. On reaching the Choke, a particularly narrow passage, which ran straight as an arrow for half a mile and at its deepest point was no more than forty metres across and overhung with juts of rock bristling with dense, snow-covered undergrowth, the wind-speed dropped significantly and the Lifeboat proceeded at a crawl.

Sometimes in the Choke – as on this occasion – progress would slow so much that the crew needed to disembark, run ahead in their snow-shoes and take up tow-lines. This was never quite as tough a call for the men as it looked; the snow was smooth and the vessel, which usually had momentum, slid easily. Beyond the Choke, the lines were drawn in again and the men scampered back on board – just in time for the southerly wind, raging down the flatter northern slopes of the Crest, to fill the sails again and kick the craft forward, the dark bulwark of the Tundra-Vald now looming several miles ahead.

They bolted towards it along a straight line delineated by Yalala Gluck's homeward-bound tracks, which, though partly obliterated by the recent snowfall, were still visible from the Lifeboat prow as rounded ruts in the moonlight. As they reached the outskirts of the trees, the tailwind slackened and they covered the final few hundred metres at a declining rate of knots.

'We'll be stopping soon,' Caleb called, checking his wind chart. 'We've an hour's deadfall due. So from here we're on foot.'

'We'll be fine,' the Doctor replied, scanning the encroaching darkness of the trees and adding under his breath: 'I don't think we'll have far to go.'

'Reef sails!' Caleb shouted, the crew hastening to obey.

Directly in front of them, the Tundra-Vald swung open like a pair of black/green curtains, and a snowy clearing roughly the size of a football field was revealed. As they cruised slowly into the midst of it, the Doctor could already see that things weren't as they should be.

The vessel slowed to a final halt, aided by the furling of its sails. The crew assembled on deck, armed with those few weapons they'd brought. The gangplank was lowered over the port gunwale, and they clumped down it in single file, eyes scanning the smooth whiteness on all sides. As the plain between the Tundra-Vald and Fafnir's Crest had revealed traces of Yalala's flight, so this clearing revealed traces of something else, numerous dints in the surface hinting at a protracted scuffle. A faint but arcing impression implied that Tiberius's dog-sled had made an abrupt turn-around, presumably when Yalala was seeking to escape.

The Doctor now gazed into a tree at the curious objects he'd spotted before they'd arrived: several strands of tattered silk, along with a mess of cords, dangling through the boughs. When he glanced further afield, he spotted similar rags and tatters hanging in other trees.

'What are these?' Luca asked, sounding fascinated and frightened at the same time.

Blond-haired and fresh-faced, Luca was the youngest member of the Lifeboat crew – he'd only been inducted this last year and had no experience yet of life outside Christmas.

'Parachutes,' the Doctor explained, as the crew gathered. 'Ingenious.' He thumbed at his chin. 'They can't batter their way through the Papal force field with their interstellar engines, so they simply drop through it instead. Who'd have thought? Mind you, it's roughly four hundred miles from the top of Trenzalore's exosphere down to the planet surface. That's quite a journey, most of which must have been spent in freefall – wouldn't fancy trying it myself. Ah-ha…'

He'd spotted something else a dozen metres to their left, and plodded quickly over there. Only part of it was visible, angling up through the snow, though when they glanced around, other half-concealed pieces could be discerned. They resembled fragments of a large eggshell, which in the pale moonlight looked to be covered in ceramic tiles, most of these cracked and blackened. The

Doctor squatted and scraped away more snow.

'Five feet in length, three to four feet in diameter around its middle when intact…' He hunkered lower to peek inside, seeing nothing but a clean metallic inner-surface. 'No controls, no insulation… no comforts of any sort.' He sniffed at the air. 'It's a cold night of course, but not a whiff to suggest chemical or biological components. A fire-proofed container then. A simple parcel… delivered by a very unwelcome cosmic postman.'

'There are more over here!' someone called.

'There'll be quite a few more I'd imagine,' the Doctor said. 'This will be one of the capsules in which they were first put into orbit.'

'Who was put into orbit?' Caleb asked.

The Doctor stuck his hands into his trouser pockets. 'Whoever it was landed here. Necessary, I suppose… especially after that orbit started to decay and they passed down through the ionosphere, or they'd have completely burned up. Did quite a bit of damage anyway, I'd expect – the capsules probably broke apart on entering the thermosphere, from which point their passengers were completely unshielded.'

'You're telling us these beings literally dropped from space?' Caleb asked.

The Doctor nodded. 'Amazing, isn't it, how the simplest methods are sometimes the best. Also explains how they finished up so far off course. Trenzalore's crosswinds take some getting used to.'

'But that's impossible.'

'For you or me, certainly. But it's astonishing what you can achieve when you don't feel any pain.'

The small group regarded the Doctor in stunned silence.

'So… so you *do* know who they are?' Caleb finally asked.

'I have theories,' the Doctor replied, 'but let's not get side-tracked, eh? We're here to find Tiberius Gluck, not spook ourselves rotten with crazy guesswork. Now… we've come from the south, so we know there's currently no one there who shouldn't be. That only leaves the other three points of the compass. So… Yoshua and Rubin, you go north. Josef and Jerema, you go west, Caleb and I will go east. Luca, that leaves you to guard the Lifeboat. Probably best to stand at the top of the gangplank. That way you'll have an advantage over anyone who comes up it towards you.'

The boy, who was only armed with the homemade spear he normally used for ice-fishing, looked more than a little nervous. 'Doctor… if these people, whoever they are… if they can't feel pain?'

'It doesn't sound good, I'll admit,' the Doctor said, 'but contrary to popular mythology, Luca, no kind of resistance is ever futile.'

'But… I mean…' The boy could still only stutter. 'If they look exactly like you…'

'No problems there, at least.' The Doctor grinned his boyish grin. 'These chaps have just nosedived through several hundred miles of thickly layered, radioactive gases, not to mention all manner of tumultuous storm systems. So you can be sure of one thing, Luca: none of them are going to look *exactly* like me. Not any more. Right…' He rubbed his hands together. 'We'll search in an expanding circle, but if we reach the point where we're out of sight of each other, we stay in contact by blowing horns, am I understood?'

They nodded grimly.

'We have approximately forty-nine minutes before the deadfall ends and the evening northerly provides us with a fast ride home. We don't want to miss that boat, do we?'

They shook their heads.

'So what are we waiting for? Let's find Tiberius Gluck.'

They found him.

Ten minutes later.

In the next clearing.

He was seated against a pine-trunk, partially covered in snow, his pack a few feet to one side of him. Fortunately, it was Yoshua, the oldest and hardiest member of the crew, who located the scrawny old prospector and shook his shoulder to see if he could revive him – to be met by a head lolling sideways on a neck so broken it was more like rubber than muscle, and a face beaten to unrecognisable ruin.

No sooner had the rest of the party closed in, the Doctor foremost among them – face etched with a deep, angry frown – than they found another body. Luca gave a shrill cry and pointed up into the next tree.

This second figure bore the basic outline of a man, and indeed wore pieces of clothing, along with a leather harness from which various cords dangled. But it appeared to have shattered on contact with the higher boughs of the moon-pine, because numerous fragments of it were scattered down through the lower branches. The upper-right quarter of its torso – still with arm and head attached – was suspended upside down near the bottom, and gruesomely distorted, its head twisted right the way around, all the hair burned from its blistered scalp.

The Doctor stepped forward to peer into its face, which just vaguely resembled his own, though both eyes had exploded from their sockets, while one whole half of it had rippled and bubbled into a scabrous horror.

'Is this… is this one of them?' Caleb said, appalled.

'I'm afraid so,' the Doctor replied.

'It looks… artificial.'

'It *is* artificial,' the Doctor said, 'though such a word doesn't really do justice to a cold, unfeeling mannequin, which in normal times would be animated to murderous action by the telekinetic powers of a very unpleasant and vindictive alien life form.'

'But what is it?'

'They have many different names, Caleb, in various different solar systems. But in the world of your forefathers, we knew them simply as… Autons.'

Chapter 5

'You don't need to look so worried, Caleb,' the Doctor said, kneeling as he rooted through Tiberius Gluck's pack, pulling out an assortment of curios, of which mess tins, trenching tools, fish hooks and several boxes of matches were the only things instantly recognisable. 'I told you, the Nestene Consciousness doesn't have a natural form. Wherever it's housed itself, it will most likely be in orbit somewhere. Probably a spaceship it's hijacked by use of other Autons. And they are all you're ever likely to see of it.'

Caleb didn't seem hugely reassured by that. He glanced again at the mangled object hanging in the tree. Rubin guarded it, crossbow nervously levelled, while Yoshua prowled the perimeter of the clearing, and Josef and Jerema were busy installing Tiberius's body, now wrapped in blankets, into the hold of the Lifeboat.

'You're sure it's dead?' Caleb asked.

'Strictly speaking, it was never alive. But it's clearly no longer viable, so it's been abandoned – nothing more now than a lump of inert polymer.'

'I thought you said these things were invulnerable?'

The Doctor was briefly distracted as he extricated a single tube of pale, malleable material from Gluck's pack. It was wrapped in thin brown paper with a greasy texture. When he sniffed at it, he detected ammonium nitrate and perhaps a hint of nitroglycerine. 'Boronite, eh?'

This was a standard industrial explosive in Earth's more far-flung colonies – about nine times stronger than ordinary dynamite, but with reduced nitroglycerine content to suppress its volatility. Even someone who routinely appeared to have made bad choices in life, like Tiberius Gluck, could handle it in relative safety.

'We had a stockpile of it during the early days of the settlement,' Caleb said. 'It was used to shot-fire through the bedrock under the town, to reach the hot springs there. The leftovers got shelved. Later on, Tiberius took some for his own use.'

'Well… boronite's always a blast.' The Doctor tucked the explosive under his coat, and rummaged deeper into the pack, producing a rolled-up length of fuse, about ten or twelve feet in total. 'On the subject of the Autons, Caleb… I don't exactly recall saying they were invulnerable. But let's face it; nothing can plummet clear through a planet's atmosphere without it doing at least some damage. It's interesting, though…' He glanced up, thoughtful. 'Perhaps the force field is interfering in some way? Maybe that and the extreme conditions on Trenzalore are limiting the Nestene's abilities. I mean, I've known plenty of Autons in my time. Most of them could change their features on the hoof, repair extensive physical damage…'

'So why isn't this creature pulling itself back together

right now?' Caleb asked.

'Exactly my point! And that's probably the good news.'

'You say that as if there's bad news too.'

'Well of course there is.' The Doctor levered himself to his feet. 'Yin and yang remember. Can't have one without the other… at least, I can't seem to.' He paused again. 'The bad news is that young Yalala Gluck was right. The Autons have always been at their most effective when used as facsimiles, disguised as people of authority. Quite a cool notion actually… if it wasn't so downright villainous. They simply replace those people in whichever community they're seeking to infiltrate. Once installed, the potential for them to cause havoc is rather high, as you can imagine. So if only one of this landing party gets through to Christmas, and it even vaguely resembles me, we've got real problems.'

'And that's where they've gone, you think?'

'Almost certainly. The main question is… how many are there?'

'No more than five, I'd say,' Yoshua interrupted, ambling towards them. 'There are tracks over here.' They followed him to the far side of the clearing, where a relatively recently trail, now little more than a set of rounded grooves, led away from the trees towards the distant ridge of Fafnir's Crest.

'You can tell there are five of them from this?' the Doctor said.

Yoshua nodded. He was the burliest member of the Lifeboat crew, and certainly possessed the most impressive beard. As well as his duties on the boat, he'd inherited the mantle of head huntsman from his father;

in times when food supplies were low, it was Yoshua they dispatched to the Outland to bring back snow-chucks, ballyblots and long-eared tundra stag. If he said these tracks had been made by five individuals, there was no reason to disbelieve him. In fact, it made a kind of sense.

'If the Nestene's control is limited on this planet, there are bound to be restrictions on the numbers of Auton units it can command,' the Doctor said. 'I mean, that's even the case on planets where conditions are good. I've never yet seen legions of Autons in action… though I did know an Auton once who was a legionary. I think.' He frowned, confused. 'Memories fade, sadly. Anyway, you and Yalala Gluck are probably right, Yoshua – we're only dealing with a handful of them. And that's got to be good. How long before the next wind, Caleb?'

Caleb checked his time-dial. 'Twelve minutes.'

'That's not so good. We'll be cutting it very close.'

'Why are they heading straight south?' Luca wondered, indicating the tracks, which, thanks to the bright moonlight, they could see ran straight as a ribbon towards the distant ridge, not veering off to the west in the direction of the Devil's Elbows or east towards the Goat Path. 'Isn't that the wrong way?'

'Not if you're heading to Christmas by the quickest route,' the Doctor said, hobbling back across the clearing.

The others followed. 'But they'd have to climb over Fafnir's Crest!' Luca argued.

'What have I said about the Autons you don't yet understand, Luca?' the Doctor replied. 'I told you, they never get tired and they have no feelings. They can march over any obstruction you put in their path.'

Caleb and Yoshua glanced at each other uneasily. The

same brief image had flickered into both their thoughts: of five tall, powerful figures, each one battered, broken, partially melted, clad in ragged remnants of clothes, yet plunging effortlessly through the drifts – knee-deep, maybe thigh-deep – but never stopping, ploughing ever forward, the escarpment drawing closer and closer, and when that arrived, simply climbing up it tirelessly, tier after tier, ledge after ledge.

'What kind of weapons do they have?' Yoshua asked.

'They normally kill with concentrated energy bolts,' the Doctor said. 'Of course, they won't have that capability on Trenzalore. Couldn't get it past the Papal Mainframe scanners.'

'From the looks of Gluck, they strangled and beat him,' Caleb said.

'Yes, well…' The Doctor tried to sound less discomforted than this made him feel. 'At least that means you guys can stand up and fight them. When you get back to town, make sure everyone bars their doors and windows. It won't be easy hammering through those with bare plastic…'

'When *we* get back to town?' Luca said. 'Are you not coming with us?'

The Doctor turned to face them. 'Of course I am.' He gave a half-smile. 'At some point. First, I want to have a go at sailing the Lifeboat. I've always fancied that.' He strode on.

The group exchanged further bewildered glances as they followed.

'So when and where are we splitting up?' Caleb asked.

'When we get to Fafnir's Crest,' the Doctor replied. 'I'll take the Lifeboat helm, and drop you off at the foot of the Goat Path. From there on, you're walking.' He slapped Caleb's shoulder. 'You're sturdy young men. You've got Yoshua to lead you. You've got your thermals on. I'm pretty sure you can make it back. In the meantime, once we get aboard, I want you to hoist the mainsail only, you understand?'

'What if we don't make it?' Caleb asked.

'Well…' The Doctor's smile faltered. 'I'm rather afraid you're going to have to. It's just possible you guys may be the townsfolk's only hope.'

Worried glances were again exchanged. The crew knew better than to question the Doctor – they'd been raised from childhood on that very understanding, despite his occasional moments of insanity – and yet now he was abandoning them?

'These Autons have a head start,' Yoshua said. 'Even if we sail to the Goat Path, that's still far to the east of here. We won't gain much ground on them, if any. And they don't get tired, remember. They'll reach Christmas long before we do.'

'They won't, Yoshua,' the Doctor replied. 'I'll do my level best to ensure that.'

'So, you're not leaving us?' Luca asked querulously. 'You're not running away?'

'I never run away, Luca. Ever.'

Luca smiled, but swallowed nervously.

'I don't understand,' Caleb said, treating the Doctor to a searching gaze. 'After you've "dropped us off", as you call it, where will you be taking the Lifeboat?'

The Doctor shrugged. 'Where else? Into the Devil's Elbows.'

'Running under a single sail, there's no chance you'll

get through the Choke at any kind of speed. Even in a strong southerly, you'll barely be moving.'

'I know.' The Doctor's face broke into a beaming grin; he poked the suspicious helmsman in the ribs. 'And isn't that the whole genius of it?'

Chapter 6

An hour later, with the evening southerly howling at full force, the crew were even less enthused about bailing out from the Lifeboat.

It was perhaps understandable. Though they were all young, energetic men, and though they were well equipped and had Yoshua to guide them over the scant trail that was the Goat Path, they still had two or three extremely difficult days ahead as they trekked back through the Outland. And of course, when they finally returned to Christmas, none of them knew what they would find there.

The Doctor was occupied at the helm as the Lifeboat tacked jerkily westward along the southern edge of Fafnir's Crest, his fur coat flapping around him. The shelter provided by the ridge had reduced the wind significantly, so they were travelling at maybe eighteen knots when, one by one, the men, now bundled in as much fur and fleece as they could manage, threw their skis and survival packs from the starboard gunwale, and jumped after them, legs hugged to chests so they would hit and roll in the snow with minimum impact.

Each one appeared to make it unscathed, springing to his feet in the Lifeboat's rear, and scampering to reclaim his equipment.

Caleb went last, but turned when he was astride the gunwale. 'You sure you can manage this vessel alone, Doctor?' he called.

The Doctor was clamped two-handed to the wheel, the manipulation of which was a tougher job than he'd expected. This simple device controlled huge forces, he realised. Deep vibrations juddered through the complex mechanisms below deck: the sheaves, the pulleys, the rudder bars and tiller ropes, not to mention the steering shaft to which the frontal skis' axle was connected. 'I'll be fine!' he shouted back.

'I think I know you well enough, Doctor,' Caleb replied. 'You wouldn't be making us walk back if the route you'd chosen wasn't even more dangerous.'

'Just get to the town, Caleb! Forget me, forget the Lifeboat… and don't even think about working your way along the top of the Crest to the Devil's Elbows. You avoid that place like the plague, you hear?'

'Surely it's better we fight the Autons out here than in the town?'

'If all goes to plan, you won't be fighting them at all… but even the best laid plans can fail if people don't stick to them. Now go!'

Caleb went, dropping his pack and his skis over the side, then vanishing after them through a swirling slipstream of flakes.

The Doctor concentrated hard on the glistening white landscape ahead, though the right side of it lay black in the shadow of the Crest. He hoped he'd be able to see the entrance to the Devil's Elbows when he finally came upon it, which, by Caleb's calculation, would be in about twenty minutes' time. Even when he reached it, he'd be relying more on luck than skill to tack through the narrow, Z-shaped passage, though it was some consolation that he only had to travel through it to the midway point, to the Choke – where those waiting to ambush him would almost certainly seek to come aboard.

The Doctor smiled grimly.

As soon as he'd realised what they were up against, he'd also understood their plan.

The planet Trenzalore had no value to the Nestene. It was a pristine wilderness, almost entirely unpolluted. There were no toxins or chemicals in its air, no acids, no metals, no smoke. Likewise, the Nestene had no real interest in Christmas or the people who lived there. This Auton hit squad was here for exactly the same reason as the numerous other intruders, who by various ruses had attempted to enter the settlement over the last three centuries.

The Doctor himself.

In the first instance, the Nestene had sought to parachute their mindless Autons onto Christmas itself, their plan simply to grab their target and bear him away to his death. With the Autons virtually indestructible against weapons fashioned out of farm tools, there'd have been nothing anyone could to prevent that. But when the furious crosswinds had blown them off course, the Nestene – always able to improvise – had formed another plan, realising the Doctor would seek to discover them and thus laying an elaborate trap.

His thoughts were distracted as he steered into the canyon; a less complex procedure than he'd anticipated, the beautifully designed craft swerving gracefully through the gap, the mainsail swivelling on its gooseneck and catching the full thrust of the southerly wind, which was funnelled and thus propelled the Lifeboat forward with even greater velocity.

'You're a lovely piece of work,' the Doctor said, fondly patting the wheel's varnished spokes. 'I am sooo sorry.'

For a brief time, the canyon's broad slopes were luminous in the double-strength radiance of Soror and Frater, the moon-pines on the ascending slopes little more than cones of frosted snow. He'd be enjoying the scenery more, though, if he wasn't at least a little bit nervous about what lay ahead – and right on cue, the Lifeboat's speed reduced as the canyon wind started dissipating over the flanks of the encircling hills. By the time they reached the Choke, some ten minutes beyond the first of the 'elbows', they'd be travelling very slowly indeed. That had to be the point where the ambushers would strike – it was the only place between the town and the Tundra-Vald where man-size bipeds had any hope of boarding the vessel.

'Well… let's see how you do, boys,' the Doctor said. 'More to the point, let's see how I do.' Because he had to get there first.

On skimming around the first of the canyon's ultra-sharp bends, the Lifeboat slid briefly out of control, listing to port as he jerked the wheel too suddenly, the frontal skis travelling sideways – before it righted itself and took off again, now along the innermost channel, the valley sides closing in, deadening all sound. The encroaching valley walls were suddenly sheer rock faces, riven with ice-packed fissures and hung with snow-caked moon-pines. The light of the two moons steadily diminished, creating a dark, tunnel-like atmosphere, though there was still sufficient passage for the mainsail to drive the craft onward at a decent twelve knots.

It might be narrow, but from here on, for half a mile or more, it was dead straight. Even so, the Doctor knew he'd have to work quickly.

'OK, steady as you go...' he said, locking off the wheel, grabbing his stick and clumping down from the bridge to the fore-hatch, which he descended through awkwardly, closing and bolting the hatch doors behind as he went.

It was much warmer in the hold, the various bunks crammed with blankets, the stove effervescing heat. There was a rich scent of percolating coffee, which unfortunately he had no time to sample at present. The door on his left led through to the Steerage Room, a large, bell-shaped cavity made from solid cast-iron, down the middle of which the central steering-shaft descended before connecting with the complex mass of rods, springs and axles that formed the Lifeboat's undercarriage, and through the midst of which there now came a grinding roar of ice and a constant spray of fresh-churned snow, which crusted the curved inner walls and rapidly feathered the Doctor from head to foot.

He forged his way through this to the end of the wire-framed pulpit, from where he could reach the upper section of the shaft. Even in his thick mittens, the Doctor's fingers were almost too numb to perform the delicate operation at hand. He had to be especially careful taking the tube of boronite from his inner coat pocket – it was the only one, and dropping it out the bottom of the boat would be a disaster. It was a pity he didn't have more of these, he reflected as he inserted the needle end of the fuse into its pliable base. But even if he had half a dozen, while that would be enormously potent – powerful enough to demolish an entire block of flats back on Earth – it might be too powerful to have the desired effect here. If a single explosive detonated, however, the bell-shaped iron of the steerage housing ought to contain much of the blast and direct it downward.

Only that way could the Doctor be certain of success – or so he hoped.

He leaned from the pulpit, braced the explosive against the metal shaft and bound the fuse around it until it was securely in place. He then wound the other end of the fuse around the tip of his stick and reaching upward, was just able to wiggle it through the narrow circular gap at the top of the shaft. When he withdrew the stick, the fuse was drawn off it like a sock and left tangled in the gap overhead.

He checked his watch – they'd reach the Choke imminently. Hurriedly, he blundered back into the hold, where he set about folding the rugs and blankets in the bunks into human outlines, and covering them with quilts.

Would the Autons be fooled?

'They're mindless lumps of plastic… Course they'll be fooled!' he answered himself.

But there was always that element of doubt. The

Nestene's control wasn't so weak. As often in the past, the Doctor realised he was winging it – taking a chance. But in truth, this was the *only* chance, not just for him but for the entire population of Christmas. If the Nestene successfully dispensed with him, their brutal soldiers would enter the town unimpeded, and kill every man, woman and child.

Resistance is never futile, he'd told Luca. But perhaps there were times when it would only delay the inevitable – and not for very long.

He could now sense the Lifeboat decelerating, the whistling headwind diminishing. The boat began jolting as it hit obstacles in the snow, which otherwise it would have sped over unnoticed. Clearly they'd entered the Choke. He could picture the thick, snow-caked vegetation enmeshed overhead. Thankfully, the Lifeboat continued forward, slithering rather than skating – but remaining in motion.

And making an irresistible target.

'Time, boys,' he said, moving to the foot of the fore-hatch ladder. 'Time.'

He imagined them leaping from overhead, one after another, like commandos, crashing down amid twigs and leafage and showers of powdery snow.

And indeed the first impacts now sounded, the thuds of heavy, bloodless bodies landing on deck.

Chapter 7

'One – two – three…' The Doctor's eyes roved left to right across the arched ceiling. 'Four…'

There was nothing further.

He felt a pang of unease. Only four? Yoshua had expected five.

Thud.

The Doctor spun around. The last one had come down at the prow – clumsily, as if it had caught in the rigging first. Confused moments followed as further movements sounded: a shuffling and thumping of heavy feet, the Autons turning, searching the deserted deck and gradually homing in on the one hatch that was still open – the aft-hatch. They advanced on it with a trudging, lifeless tread.

Timber creaked as weight bore down on the top rung. The Doctor scrambled quickly up his own ladder to the fore-hatch. As he did, from the corner of his eye he glimpsed something twisted and tattered descending into view at the far end of the hold. A similar something was directly behind it.

Deftly as he could, he drew the bolts, lifted the hatch

and levered himself out, closing the doors quietly behind him – and keeping low. From here, the aft-hatch was partly screened by the bridge, but he could still see the last of the raiding party – a broken, lop-sided shape in the glacial dimness, stooping down as it descended into the hold. The last part of it to vanish from sight was its left hand, in which it clasped a gnarled, knotty branch.

A club.

Autons with clubs.

Briefly, that seemed more terrifying than Autons with built-in blasters.

He remained crouched, waiting with bated breath – until a frantic hammering and crashing commenced below deck, the Autons attacking the covered forms.

Jolted into action, the first thing he dealt with was the fore-hatch. It wasn't possible to lock it from above, but it possessed two ring-pull handles, which he jammed together by thrusting a stainless steel spar through them. For good measure, he unlocked one of the supply barrels fixed in a rack along the port gunwale. Emergency supplies in the event of the Lifeboat becoming marooned, these were crammed to capacity with salt pork, salt fish or hardtack biscuit, so it took as much determination as strength to manoeuvre the ungainly thing across the deck and place it on top of the closed hatch.

The chaos below was still ear-shattering. For creatures composed entirely of unfeeling plastic, the Autons were unleashing a demonic rage against their would-be victims. More than a little disconcerted by this, the Doctor hobbled along the deck to the aft-hatch, closed that as well, then pulled down a control line from the overhanging boom, tied it around the handles in the closest approximation he could muster to a constrictor knot, and threaded it through a porthole on the starboard gunwale, where he tied it off.

Of course, the hatch doors were made of wood – nothing more. The Autons would smash their way back up to the deck in due course. How long it would take them was anyone's guess.

The Doctor limped up onto the bridge, and released the wheel.

Only now did he notice how slowly they were travelling – a couple of knots max. The mainsail barely fluttered overhead. But at least there was moonlight looming, the Choke finally broadening out. He glanced enviously at the other sails, all neatly packaged away. Even if he knew how to unfurl them effectively, there was only one of him – it wouldn't be possible to do it.

Instead, he took hold of the wheel, teeth gritted.

A cacophony still raged below, and yet it noticeably dwindled as, slowly and dully, the Autons realised they had been duped. Perhaps a minute later, those clubs began battering on the undersides of the hatches.

Still the vessel slid laboriously on.

'Any time you're ready,' the Doctor shouted, glancing up at the drooping mainsail.

But it was another fifty metres before the cliff-sides folded back properly, and the mainsail started rippling again – and then bellying. The Doctor didn't whoop for joy just yet. The Lifeboat was accelerating, but only slowly. Meanwhile, ponderous blows still stuck the undersides of the hatches, growing steadily in force and ferocity. Even so, he was relieved to feel that vibration in the base of the steering mechanism. When the wheel lugged to starboard, he had to lean on it hard. The Lifeboat's speed increased, the landscape swooping by, snowflakes swirling. Twelve to fifteen knots, he estimated. Steadily faster, fifteen to twenty – this was more like it.

They spun around the second elbow at ever-increasing pace, the craft again skidding, the boom swinging wildly, the Doctor hanging hard to port, and now – less than a mile ahead, he saw the great V-shaped gap at the south end of Devil's Elbows canyon.

Beyond that lay the open plains, at the far side of which, some thirty miles away, stood the town. But they weren't going that far, or even in that direction.

Their destination, though he hadn't disclosed this to the others – you could never be totally sure there weren't already facsimiles among you – lay due west, and no sooner had the vessel burst out into the open space, than the Doctor saw it: a vast, perfectly horizontal glimmer of reflected starlight, spreading north and south as far as the eye could see.

Lake Lagda.

It was still several minutes away, but the southerly was strengthening even more, driving the craft with fury. The Doctor glanced down over the wheel. Even under the barrel, the fore-hatch was cracking and splitting in its frame. A blackened fist punched through its centre.

'No thank you!' Doctor yelled. He hopped from the bridge, grabbed one of the crew's homemade spears and jammed it down through the splintered aperture – again and again, with vicious force, striking his target repeatedly, inflicting no pain and yet hopefully hindering it. He only needed a couple of minutes more;

that was all. But his foe proved unyielding beneath the taped blade, and grappled strenuously with the weapon, finally catching the shaft and snapping it in half.

A similar *crunch* of timber echoed from the aft-hatch.

The Doctor glanced around, white-faced – only for the swishing of snow beneath the Lifeboat's runners to transform into a harsh rattle, and the jolting and juddering of their passage to abruptly cease. Suddenly they were running smoothly, and at incredible speed.

The Doctor tottered to the gunwale. A gleaming mirrored surface swept away in all directions. He glanced to the rear, where the moonlit shore receded fast.

He laughed aloud as he limped back to the wheel, dropped onto his haunches and grabbed the fuse he'd threaded up through the gap around the wheel's base. Next, he filched a box of Tiberius Gluck's matches from his pocket – only to find that it was no easy thing striking them in this blizzard. One after another, three matches snapped without catching – four, five, six. And now, with a crash and clatter, the barrel was cast aside, and the Doctor sensed an immense figure struggling to ascend past the steel spar.

'Come on, come on!' he muttered.

The seventh, eighth and ninth matches snapped as well – and now there were only a couple left. But the tenth caught, issuing a fast, blue spurt, which he touched to the end of the fuse. It hissed to life, as the Doctor pivoted to his feet and stumbled to the starboard gunwale, throwing his good leg over it and – with a wild shout of 'Gernominoooo!' – dragging his wooden one after him.

Landing on ice at such velocity was something he

hadn't totally planned for.

It hit him like a sledgehammer, sending shudders of pain and nausea through his entire body. He rolled for maybe thirty metres, a mass of ungainly limbs, banging and bouncing on the rock-solid surface, and sliding face-down for another twenty, before staring groggily up after the fast diminishing Lifeboat.

The flash as its bottom section blew out was blinding.

A thunderclap detonation followed, burning splinters gusting in every direction, swamping the Doctor as he lay with his head wrapped in his arms. Beneath him, the frozen lake shuddered – and then fractured, fissures racing every which way. In fact, the next thing the Doctor knew, he was lying on a floating slab, which promptly tilted left, freezing water slopping over his left arm. He clutched on hard, fingertips dug into the glacial surface, before it slowly righted itself again.

All around him lay a sea of jostling ice-cakes, each one cast in a fiery glow by the orange flames erupting through the charred shell of the Lifeboat, which had come to a halt about eighty metres away and now sagged downward, prow-first.

The Doctor watched it tensely, willing it to disappear. Surely it would?

The weight of that undercarriage – there had to be some of it still attached – surely that mass of tangled, twisted steel would pull it down?

With a loud gurgling, the vessel began to sink properly, its stern rising upward, exposing edges of ragged, smouldering timber where its keel had once been.

Hope surged in the Doctor's breast, but now the

question nagged at him – could the Autons swim? He supposed that depended on how burned and dismembered they were after the blast. Even if they weren't in such a state, they were solid plastic and far too heavy to float, and Lake Lagda was monstrously deep – a geological fault rather than a flooded valley, dropping thousands and thousands of feet with sheer mud walls at its sides. As he watched the wreck, the flames inside it rapidly dwindled, now doused by an inward-pouring tide, until they winked out in a puff of smoke, leaving the vessel little more than a broken, blackened outline. Once again, silver moonlight provided the only illumination. The Doctor knelt upright, his scalp prickling as the Lifeboat's stern halted above the surface. His ice slab wobbled precariously, but for several seconds he barely noticed this – and then the wreck sank downward again.

He almost allowed himself to relax – until he spotted something else.

A figure had appeared at the stern, perched like an ape on the rearmost gunwale.

Even as this last fragment of woodwork vanished beneath the roiling surface, the lanky form sprang away, landing lithely on an ice fragment, rocking it from side to side. And then sprang again. Nimble as a frog, it landed on all fours on a second ice fragment.

'You cannot be serious,' the Doctor said slowly.

In three bounds, it had come almost thirty metres closer to him.

It leapt a fourth time, again landing successfully. It was even closer now. What nightmare parody of himself would this one present, he wondered? First it had dropped through the atmosphere, and now it had been blown up and seared by flame. There wouldn't be much remaining of his wholesome Gallifreyan features.

With a fifth and truly prodigious leap, it reached another fragment, this time hitting the frozen surface with an audible *thud*, and landing off-centre – to such a degree the slab tipped sideways. The black shape of the Auton clung to it spread-eagled, but the slab continued to overbalance, halting briefly upright, before flipping all the way over, its rugged brown underside glistening in the starlight.

'Ahhh, well… hard cheese.' The Doctor prodded himself upright with his stick. 'Dancing on ice isn't for everyone. The best laid plans and all that.'

He pivoted around, the bitter wind lashing across him, frost tendrils materialising even as he watched in the sodden fur of his coat's left sleeve. His left hand felt raw and numb. Chilblains, he thought wonderingly. First time for everything on Trenzalore. On the upside, the terrible cold meant it wouldn't be long before the shattered surface solidified again, allowing him to limp back to shore. He stamped a couple of times, tapped the ice with his stick. Definitely melding itself back together.

That was when the Auton exploded up from the water on his right.

It was anyone's guess how it had traversed the final fifty metres beneath the surface. Possibly clambering over other sunken ice chunks; maybe hooking its nerveless fingers into their filth-clotted undersides. But, with a *whoosh* of slush and muck, it now landed with arms spread on the right side of the Doctor's own private island, lop-siding it so spectacularly that the Doctor had to throw himself onto his backside to rebalance it.

Up close, the mannequin was every inch the horror he'd imagined: a mangled, contorted effigy. Not a scrap of clothing remained, not a strand of hair, not a hint of facial feature amid the brutish lumps of scorched plastic – save for a single eye, partly dislodged from its sole remaining orbit but fixed on him with laser-like intensity.

The Nestene's eye.

Several times battling the Autons, he'd been confronted with the Nestene's eye; usually it was artificial and yet always it had provided a clear window to the soulless malignancy that lurked underneath.

It was the eye where the Doctor attacked.

In truth, he didn't know whether the imitation organ was just for effect, or actually served to transmit vision to the hideous intellect in the realm beyond. But it seemed as good a place as any – so he slid forward on his knees and jabbed sword-like with his stick, jolting the organ out on some kind of synthetic thread. The Auton, still braced with both hands, could not respond. So he jabbed a second time, and now the eye came loose entirely. But this didn't stop the Auton raising its right knee onto the slab, and as the centre of its balance changed, snatching at the stick and catching hold.

The Doctor yanked the implement back – it was sheathed with ice and slid from the Auton's grasp. And when he next struck, it was with both hands, smashing it into the side of the monster's head, first from the left and then the right.

But Doctor, these beings feel no pain.

With both knees now on board, it rose towards its feet. The ice tilted again. The Doctor slipped sideways.

It was a narrow gap between this ice fragment and the next, but was filled with black, slushy water and wide enough to swallow him whole. He scrambled madly backward, coiling his good leg beneath him, and catapulting himself upward – hitting his opponent with a massive body-check just as it reached full height.

The Auton was sturdy enough to withstand the blow, to smother him in a bear-hug, but now the slab tilted the other way, and suddenly *both* of them were falling.

The Auton released him, but it was too late – the Doctor kicked himself into a dive, and landed full-length on the neighbouring slab, driving his stick point down to spike himself in place. The impact drove the two slabs even further apart, the fissure between them widening dramatically, and the Auton landed in this with a terrific *SPLASH*.

But it still hadn't fully released him.

Its twisted talon slid down his left trouser-leg, gaining no purchase, but fastened around his ankle. For frantic seconds, they were locked together again, the Auton half submerged and thrashing in the gelid stew, the Doctor lying sideways on the ice, the slab tilting up behind him – he began to slide.

'This is gonna be great!' he gasped, rummaging with his right hand through his multiple layers of clothes. 'Like I need this.'

At the same time, he rammed his free foot down on the Auton's burned face, again and again, hoping to cause enough of a distraction in which to locate and snap open several essential buckles – which he duly did.

Joint by joint, his artificial leg emerged from his trouser-leg cuff.

The Auton, still clinging to it, went under.

The Doctor scrabbled back from the edge, a handful of leather straps disgorging from the cuff and whipping down under the slopping surface as well. A split second later, the ice slabs banged together over the top of it.

'You think I want to have to go to all that trouble... again?' he groaned, twin hearts beating a fierce tattoo in his chest. 'Make myself a new leg?'

Almost as an afterthought, he turned onto his stomach and wormed his way to the edge of the slab, peering down through the slight gap that had reopened. Perhaps absurdly, he half expected to catch a final glimpse of the Auton's hairless head as it descended into the void. But he saw nothing – only darkness, and now even that was dimmed as new ice crystals formed and rapidly thickened.

All around him, the lake was refreezing, the polar wind billowing fresh flakes across its newly ridged surface, pasting it white. It was going to be a long walk home, he surmised, as he levered himself to his feet – or rather, a long hop.

The stuff he did, he thought resignedly, in the name of Christmas.

The Dreaming
by Mark Morris

Chapter 1

He was being strangled. He could feel something round his neck, getting tighter and tighter. But when he put his hands up to his throat, there was nothing there. Only his fingernails scraping at his own skin.

Where was he? In a dark place, that was all he knew. The darkness had a texture to it, like oil. He felt that if he moved quickly it would slide across his flesh, slick and cold.

Not that he *could* move quickly. He could barely move at all. His head was pounding; his eyes felt hot in his swollen face; his lungs laboured for air.

He clawed at his neck again, then dropped to his knees. He sensed that this was a terrible place. A place of fear and madness and cruelty and aching, eternal loss.

Was that a breath on the back of his neck? Or perhaps the brush of fingertips? *Help me*, he tried to say, but couldn't get even a croak past his constricted throat.

His head swam. He felt consciousness ebbing. The blackness from outside was seeping in, obliterating his thoughts…

Then suddenly the pressure around his throat was

gone. He had the impression of something uncoiling, slithering away. He fell forward, gasping, choking, suddenly – *wonderfully* – able to breathe again.

'Unpleasant, isn't it, being reminded how fragile you are? How easily you could be reduced to nothing?'

The voice was icy, spiteful, and it seemed to possess an unpleasant tinkling quality, as though the words it spoke were accompanied by the faint sound of shattering glass.

He massaged his aching throat. Gingerly, still on his knees, he turned his head.

A man stood there. White-skinned. Sepulchral. His eyes burning.

He was dressed all in black, like an undertaker.

'Who are you?'

The question was a rasping whisper, but the white-faced man sprang forward like a long-legged spider to squat beside him.

'The important thing isn't so much who *I* am, but who *you* are. What's your name?'

'Aliganza.' He tried to clear his throbbing throat. 'Aliganza Torp.'

The white-faced man raised his eyebrows. 'Are you sure about that?'

Aliganza hesitated. He couldn't honestly say he was sure about anything just now. 'I… Yes.'

'Interesting,' said the white-faced man.

'What is?'

'Your name. I mean, that's not what *he* calls you, is it?'

'Who?'

'You know who!'

The white-faced man's sudden anger was intense,

and Aliganza quailed. The man's eyes blazed. Viciously he snapped, '*Him!* He who shall be obeyed. The man in the high tower. The *saviour* of Christmas.'

'You mean… the Doctor?'

'The *Doctor*.'

The man's features writhed, and just for a second Aliganza saw something beneath them. Something hideous. Then the image was gone before it could imprint itself on his mind.

When the man spoke again, his voice was silky, his mouth stretching into a smile that seemed wider than it should be.

'What *does* he call you?' he asked. 'Or should I say… what *did* he call you? When you were young?'

Aliganza smiled at the memory. 'He called me Barnable. Barnable the 43rd.'

'And why was that?'

'Because… he liked me.' Despite the situation Aliganza swelled with pride. 'All the children he liked, all his favourites, he called them…'

His voice tailed off. The white-faced man was shaking his head.

'No. He didn't call you Barnable because he liked you. He called you Barnable because he *couldn't remember* your real name. Don't you see? You're nothing to him. An insect. A mere blink of his eye. He's forgotten about you already. He's ancient, and he's cold, and he doesn't care. He doesn't care one jot about anything but his own pride, his own glory.'

'No,' Aliganza muttered. 'You don't know him. He's a good man. A *great* man. He's kind and—'

'What's his name?' asked the white-faced man.

'What?'

'His name? What is it?'

'Well, it's… he's the Doctor.'

The white-faced man sneered. 'That's not a *name*. That's a *title*. You see? He thinks so little of you that he won't even tell you his name. And that's why you're all in danger, isn't it? That's why you live in constant fear? Because he's too grand, too important, to tell you his name. Such hubris. Such arrogance.'

Aliganza shook his head. 'No… it's not like that.'

'What *is* it like then?'

But Aliganza could think of nothing to say. The man's voice, his icy words, were twisting around his thoughts like tendrils of mist around the stone markers in the churchyard.

And didn't they make a kind of sense? Weren't they opening his mind to a truth he perhaps should have faced – that they *all* should have faced – generations ago?

'I have something for you,' the white-faced man said.

'What is it?'

'A gift. Hold out your hand.'

Aliganza hesitated. The man smiled. His mouth was wide, and red, and wet.

'I won't hurt you,' he said silkily. 'Hold out your hand.'

Aliganza obeyed.

'Father!'

The small boy leaped back from the bed as the man sat up with a roar. For a moment he was terrified. His father, usually so kind, looked like a monster.

Pericles Torp knew about monsters. They came to Christmas all the time. They came to kill, to destroy, and although it was scary, it was usually all right in the end because the Doctor always beat them.

However, Pericles knew that even the Doctor couldn't save everybody. When Pericles was a baby some monsters called Krotons invaded Christmas, and several people died when the invaders destroyed the grain warehouse where they were taking shelter.

The Doctor got angry and sad when people died, and he went to the families and apologised as if it was his fault, but nobody blamed him for it. They knew if it weren't for him more people would die. They knew if it weren't for him Christmas would have been destroyed a thousand times over.

People said the Doctor was hundreds of years old. Hundreds and hundreds. Pericles didn't know about that, but he did know that the Doctor was an old man now, and that he spent more and more time in the Clock Tower guarding the funny crack in the wall. And he knew that the people of Christmas were worried. Worried of what might happen if the Doctor were to…

'What do you want?'

For a moment Pericles's father's voice didn't sound like his at all. It sounded cold and jagged and icy. And his eyes in the gloom looked strange, as if they were glowing with yellow light.

Instinctively Pericles held up the lantern that was dangling from his hand, held it up to his father's face. His father flinched and snarled, 'What are you doing? Get away from me!' But that was all right, because the light revealed there was nothing wrong with his eyes, that Pericles had been mistaken.

'Sorry, Father,' Pericles said. 'I heard you shouting, so

I came to see what the matter was. Were you… having a nightmare?'

For a moment Aliganza Torp glared at his son, then his features softened a little.

'A nightmare?' he muttered. 'Yes… that must have been it.'

'Are you all right now?'

Aliganza nodded. 'Yes, I'm quite all right. Now go back to bed. You need your sleep. School in the morning.'

Pericles lowered the lantern. He nodded in relief. 'Yes, Father. Goodnight, Father.'

Aliganza's voice was a rumble from the shadows that swarmed over his bearded face. 'Goodnight, son.'

When he was sure that Pericles was sleeping, Aliganza padded through to the bathroom. Next to the mirror above the washbasin was an oil lamp. He lit it and looked at his reflection.

His eyes were not his own. They were yellow, the pupils nothing but vertical black slits. He recoiled with a gasp. Blinked and looked again. Then he let out the gasp in a shuddering breath of relief.

He had been mistaken. His eyes *were* his own, after all. The momentary image must have been a consequence of his dream, which lingered in his mind, like a chip of ice.

A further shudder went through him. It was cold tonight. Colder than usual. Yet his arm felt hot. And it itched. He held it up, under the light.

The skin of his right forearm was red and raised and bumpy. Some kind of rash. He scratched at it, but that only seemed to stimulate it, to send odd, tingling shocks along his veins, up through his arm and shoulder and neck, into the backs of his eyes, his mind…

He heard cold, silvery laughter. Where was it coming from?

He looked into the mirror again.

'I am Aliganza Torp,' he whispered.

He went back to bed.

Chapter 2

The Doctor was whittling. Nothing like a good whittle to focus the mind. Every so often his eye strayed to the glowing crack on the wall, but it was the same as it ever was. The same as it had been over seven hundred and fifty years ago, when he had first come to Christmas.

His body – his *final* body, and to be honest, one of his favourites – had been young then. Full of vim and vigour.

'Vim and vigour,' he muttered, liking the sound of the words. 'Vim. And vigour.'

He'd had two legs back then, of course, before that nasty business with a blind Tsunami Snake. A little bandy, perhaps, but each perfectly complementing the other. And his mind had been sharp. Sharp as a… as a…

He looked at the knife in his hand. His brow furrowed with bemusement. He didn't like knives. Nasty, cutty things. Good for spreading butter, though. And jam. On crumpets. And also good for…

Ah! Whittling! That was it. He'd been whittling.

Nothing like a good whittle to focus the… er…

'Doctor?'

The Doctor's head snapped up. There was a girl

standing beside him. She looked nervous, as most people did when they were in proximity to the crack. In fact, the adults hardly ever came here. It was only the children who sometimes came to sit, and talk, and drink cocoa, and bring him their broken toys.

He looked at the girl's anxious eyes, at her woolly red hat and her long, thick coat edged in strips of brightly coloured material.

'Hello, Amelia,' he said gently.

'It's Mellandine, Doctor,' she corrected him.

'Mellandine. Of course. What can I do for you? Jetpack for your favourite doll?' Suddenly his arm shot up and he extended a warning finger. 'If it's X-ray glasses, I'm afraid the answer's no. Got into all sorts of trouble with Mrs Pilke over those.'

'There's trouble in the village, Doctor,' she said. 'At the tavern.'

'Oh, blimey. It's not the Ice Warriors again? Big, beefy chaps, but they can't hold their mead.'

'It's Sylvian Capple, Doctor. He's... gone strange. Father said I should fetch you.'

At once the Doctor's mind snapped into place. It's how it always seemed to happen nowadays. He'd while away the days, his thoughts woolly and vague, but then at the first sign of trouble – *snap!* There he'd be, back again. The Doctor. The great protector. Ready to defend Christmas from all comers.

At times like this he wanted to leap to his feet, whip out his sonic and dash down the stairs – but where the mind was willing, the flesh was sadly weak.

As he struggled to push himself upright, his wispy white hair fluttering around his head like cobwebs, he turned to Mellandine, his saggy features crinkling into a smile.

'Have a poke around in that trunk, would you, Mellandine?' he said, nodding towards a battered travelling case, its top propped open against a wooden pillar. 'I think I'm going to need my special sheriff's hat for this one.'

Christmas was a happy place – when bits of the town weren't being blown up by invaders, that is – and the Christmas Tavern, owned and run by Mellandine's father, Fergin Eggleton, was probably the happiest place of all. It walls vibrated with bustle and laughter; they oozed with juicy gossip and tall tales and bawdy jokes. Each night the majority of the townsfolk congregated there to drink mead (mulled or otherwise) and chat about local matters.

But when the Doctor hobbled in, a laser-singed Stetson perched on his head, he was greeted not with joyous bonhomie but silent tension. All but two of the tavern's occupants were huddled against the left-hand wall, troubled, even fearful expressions on their faces.

The only two people *not* huddled against the wall were Fergin Eggleton and Sylvian Capple. Fergin, a jolly barrage balloon of a man with a bald head and a large ginger moustache, was standing in the middle of the mostly empty floor, hands raised in a calming gesture. The mop-headed form of Sylvian Capple, who Fergin was facing, was squatting against the right-hand wall, his beanpole body folded in on itself like a crumpled daddy-long-legs.

Despite his hunched position, Sylvian looked

anything but submissive. On the contrary, he resembled a coiled spring, the muscles in his thin limbs straining with tension, his red-rimmed eyes darting everywhere, his teeth clenched in a feral snarl. In his hands he gripped a small ice-pick, the curved head gleaming dully in the lamplight.

As the Doctor entered, Fergin shot him a look that was part warning and part gratitude.

The Doctor gave a single nod, and smiled at Sylvian.

'Now, Sylvian,' he said softly, 'what's all this about, eh?' He approached the man cautiously, and then, wincing with pain as his remaining knee made a popping sound, squatted in front of him. Nodding at the ice-pick he said, 'You want to be careful with that. You'll do yourself a mischief.'

Sylvian's only response was to huddle further into himself, an animal-like growl starting up in his throat.

The Doctor's eyes narrowed. 'Why so frightened? What have you seen?'

'He's been having the dreams, Doctor,' Fergin muttered behind him.

'The dreams?'

'Lots of folks been having them these last few days. Terrible dreams. Been affecting them badly, it has.'

'Has it indeed?' said the Doctor thoughtfully. He laid his walking stick on the ground, slipped his hand into the pocket of his patched and dusty overcoat and withdrew his sonic screwdriver. Turning it on, he manipulated the settings until it was pulsing with soft light. He held it up so that the light was reflected in Sylvian's eyes.

'That's it, Sylvian,' he murmured. 'Look at the pretty light. Stare deeply into it and feel your worries ebbing away.' He glanced over his shoulder, where Fergin was swaying on the spot, eyes glazing. 'Not you, Fergin.'

Turning back to Sylvian, the Doctor watched as the tension seeped from the man's hollow-cheeked face.

'There we go,' he murmured. 'Now, Sylvian, what can you tell me about these dreams you've been having?'

At once, Sylvian's eyes opened wide, and just for an instant they seemed to change, to turn yellow. With a roar he leaped forward, swinging his ice-pick at the Doctor's head.

Momentarily belying his infirmity, the Doctor threw himself backwards. His Stetson tumbled off and landed on the floor between his outstretched legs. The curved end of the pick slammed into the top of it, pinning it to the wooden floor. Snarling and drooling, Sylvian tried to wrench the pick free, but it was so deeply embedded in the hat and the floor beneath that he couldn't shift it. He jerked upright, fingers hooked into claws as if he intended to rip the Doctor apart with his bare hands.

Holding up his sonic, the Doctor adjusted the controls and a high-pitched screech filled the room. As the townsfolk clapped their hands to their ears, Sylvian's face creased in pain. With a howl he leaped over the Doctor, scampered towards the partly open door and bolted into the snow.

The Doctor turned the sonic off. For a moment nobody moved. Then townsfolk were bustling forward to help him to his feet. One of them picked up his stick and handed it to him. Others brushed at the dust on his coat.

The Doctor glanced ruefully at his Stetson, which was still pinned to the floor by the ice-pick. Then his face crunched into a scowl and he waved his hands in the air.

'I'm angry with you!' he shouted. 'Very, very angry.' He pointed accusingly at Fergin. 'A few days, you said. Why didn't anyone tell me about these dreams?'

The townsfolk shuffled back from him. Some looked down at the floor, shame-faced.

Fergin mumbled, 'We didn't want to disturb you, Doctor. You're an important man.'

The Doctor rolled his eyes. '*Important?* I'm not important. I'm the *least* important man in this town.' He waved his stick at the assembled townsfolk. 'It's you lot who are important. Haven't I told you at least a squillion times that if anything even *remotely* unusual happens, you let me know? Straight away?'

The townsfolk nodded mutely.

'Good.' The Doctor cast another rueful glance at his Stetson. Sadly he said, 'I used to have my finger on the pulse. Now I've barely even *got* a pulse.' He dropped his sonic into his pocket, then placed a gnarled hand on Fergin's shoulder. 'I'm getting old, Fergin.'

Fergin tried to laugh, but there was a troubled look in his eyes. 'Nonsense, Doctor. You've got years left in you yet. You'll outlive us all.'

The Doctor smiled wryly.

Aliganza's arm was itching. He rose from sleep scratching at it, despite the fact that raking his fingernails across the reddened flesh gave him no relief at all. In fact, with each scratch, icy, tinkling pains shot up his arm and into his body, as if the blood in his veins had turned to slivers of glass.

Oddly, though, once the slivers reached his mind,

they didn't feel like pains at all; they felt like *thoughts*. They were not *his* thoughts, and yet at the same time they were. It was as if the old him – dull, slow, unambitious – was being pushed aside, and a new him – ruthless, confident, single-minded – was taking over.

He slid from his bed, feeling lithe, almost weightless, like a young man again. He stretched and breathed in the air, and it was as if he was being reborn.

There was something he needed to do. Something urgent. He didn't know what, but it nagged at him nevertheless. He felt like a puppet, as if someone was pulling his strings. But at the same time the feeling was *good*; it was *right*. It was such a relief to be relieved of his day to day worries, his constant need to put food on the table, his responsibilities towards… towards…

Pericles.

For a moment the word seemed alien to him; he had no idea what it meant. Then the information popped into his mind. Pericles. His son. Of course.

A coldness swept through him. A kind of contempt. He left the room as if compelled to do so, padded along the creaking wooden landing of his little house to a door further along the corridor.

His hand curled around the doorknob. He pushed the door open.

The boy was sleeping peacefully, his blond hair spread over his pillow.

Aliganza regarded him coldly for a moment. Then he pulled the door closed and went downstairs.

It was here, in the narrow cupboard beside the kitchen, where he kept his tools. He opened the cupboard, reached in and closed his hand around the haft of his spade.

Suddenly, Aliganza knew where he needed to go, what he needed to do.

His arm itched and itched, sending new thoughts into his brain.

He opened the door of his cottage and stepped out into the snow.

The Doctor was at the top of the Clock Tower, holding an old-fashioned brass telescope to his eye. Through it he saw a steady stream of townsfolk leaving their homes, each carrying a spade or a pick or some other digging implement. There were men and women, but no children. He pondered on this. If these townsfolk were being controlled by some malign influence then presumably either the children were immune to it (too free-spirited? Too imaginative? Too defiant?) or the infiltrator had discarded them thus far because of their lack of physical strength. Unless, as it was only a fraction of the total population that was on the move, it was just a coincidence. But the Doctor didn't believe in coincidence. Not really.

The possessed townsfolk were heading in the same direction – towards the thick woodland to the north of the town. The Doctor wondered what they were being sent to dig up. A meteor? A spaceship? A weapon?

There was only one way to find out.

'Halt!'

The man standing at the entrance to the forest was Tomalin Pilke, the schoolteacher's son. He worked in one of the large heated greenhouses on the outskirts of Christmas, which produced food and vegetables for the community. The Doctor had known Tomalin since he was a child – he'd known *everyone* in Christmas since they were children, even the town's oldest resident Vida Clatterly.

'Hello!' the Doctor called, waving a trowel enthusiastically in the air. 'I've come to help with the dig.'

Tomalin was generally a cheerful young man, but he didn't look cheerful now. His mouth was set in a thin line. And the way he was brandishing his rake, its tines pointed at the Doctor like an upraised claw, was anything but friendly.

'What do you know of the dig?' he asked.

'Oh, quite a lot,' bluffed the Doctor. 'I know that it's happening. In the woods. And that it's important. Very, very important. Vital, in fact.'

Tomalin seemed to contemplate his words. Finally he said, 'You are… the Doctor.'

'Ten out of ten for observation. Always said you were a bright boy. "Mrs Pilke," I said to your mother, "that boy of yours will go far. Recognises people just by looking at them." Sharp as a… pointy thing. So I'll just slip through, shall I?'

The Doctor hobbled forward, but Tomalin brandished the rake even more aggressively.

'You are not welcome here,' he said.

The Doctor's eyes narrowed. 'Says who?'

For a moment Tomalin looked apologetic, as if his real personality was breaking through, then his face set like granite once more. 'Leave now, before you regret it.'

Slowly the Doctor raised his stick and pointed it at the young man. 'Why don't you show your true face?' he said. 'Too scared, is that it? Too cowardly? Prefer to hide behind someone else's?'

'I do not fear you, Doctor,' hissed Tomalin.

'Yeah? Well, you *should*.'

'You are old. Weak. You are no longer a threat to us.'

The Doctor rolled his eyes. 'Blah, blah, blah. Heard it all before. Read the book, seen the film, got the T-shirt. No doubt you're too arrogant to listen to advice, but here's some anyway: leave this planet. Run or slither or scuttle away as fast as your appendages can carry you. I may be old, but you know what? That only makes me twice as dangerous. Because I don't care any more. My time is short, and if I'm gonna go out, I may as well go out fighting.'

He lowered his cane.

Tomalin did not move.

'You think about it, big boy,' the Doctor said softly. 'You think about it hard.'

Then, waving his trowel in the air one last time, he turned and ambled away.

Chapter 3

When the townsfolk emerged from their homes a couple of hours later to raise their faces to the golden sun rising briefly above the distant mountains, they were greeted not with the usual whisper of falling snow, but with clanks and thumps and what may have been Gallifreyan swearwords drifting from the upper section of the Clock Tower.

Distracted by the sounds, many turned their eyes to the tower before the sun had even set. Those that were still there five minutes later saw the Doctor, weighed down by some kind of backpack, clamber up onto the outer wall, sway for a moment, and then with a cry of, 'Geronimo!' launch himself into space.

The townsfolk screamed and gasped. A few even rushed forward, arms outstretched, as if to catch the Doctor as he fell.

But he didn't fall. Not for more than a couple of seconds anyway. Those below heard the unmistakable trill of his sonic screwdriver, and then they all gasped anew as, with a clank and a whirr, huge wings, or blades, or paddles, opened up and began to spin above the

Doctor's head.

'Whoa!' shouted the Doctor as his falling body shot upwards. For the next minute or so, he swooped and jerked above the people of Christmas like a puppet whose operator has lost control of the strings.

Eventually, however, he seemed to get the hang of the contraption, and his manoeuvres became less spasmodic, more controlled. He levelled out, and as he gained confidence he began to cut figure '8's through the sky with grace and precision, whooping delightedly. Finally, he slowed, hovered, and then, like some dishevelled messenger from on high, descended to earth.

As soon as he touched down, and the blades had folded in on themselves like the petals of a flower at night, he was surrounded by children, all of whom demanded to know how his contraption worked, or begged him to take them up into the sky. The Doctor fended them off, laughing, as Fergin plodded up to him.

'What's that thing, Doctor?' Fergin eyed the folded 'wings' warily.

'It's my whirligig,' replied the Doctor proudly. 'Do you like it?'

Fergin frowned. 'What's it for?'

'Is it a toy?' one of the children piped up.

The Doctor ruffled the child's hair. 'No, it's not a toy.' His expression became serious as he cast his gaze across the faces of the assembled adults.

'I know that many of you are worried about your loved ones,' he said. 'I know you're wondering what's wrong with them, and why the place beside you in bed was empty when you woke up this morning.'

There was a murmur of consternation. Looks were exchanged. A few heads nodded.

'Is it another one, Doctor?' someone asked.

Another one. Spoken with dread, and yet also with the weary acceptance of the constantly besieged.

The Doctor nodded apologetically. 'Yes, I'm afraid so.'

'Who is it this time?' asked Fergin.

'I'm not sure yet… though I have a nasty suspicion.' His forehead crinkled in a frown. 'Whoever they are, though, they're sneaky. A bunch of cowardly custards. They attack from the inside. Worming their way in like parasites.'

'So how's this… whirligig going to help us?' Fergin cast another wary glance at the folded blades, as if he expected them to come alive at any moment and start hacking indiscriminately at all and sundry.

The Doctor's eyes lit up. 'Ah, well, with this I can be a party pooper.'

Some of the children giggled. With evident relish one of them asked, 'What's a party *pooper?*'

'In this case, a party pooper is someone who sticks their nose in where it's not wanted.' The Doctor's face became a mass of wrinkles as he grinned. 'Which, though I say so myself, is one of the things I'm particularly good at.'

Although he knew it was childish, the Doctor gleaned an inordinate amount of pleasure from seeing the open-mouthed astonishment and rage on the face of Tomalin Pilke – or rather, the thing that was controlling Tomalin Pilke – as he whirred overhead.

'Don't mind me,' he called with a cheery wave. 'I'm just passing through.'

He made a slight adjustment on his sonic, and the motor he had constructed from the inert bits and pieces of alien technology he had secretly salvaged over the years increased in pitch. This caused the blades above his head to whirr faster and tilt at an angle that, though slight, lifted him above the tallest trees of the forest, whose spiny branches seemed to be clawing upwards through the bright moonlight to grab at his dangling legs.

He had already used his sonic as a heat sensor to find out where the dreamers had congregated, and he headed now in that direction. He knew he wouldn't be able to sneak up on them – the whirligig was too noisy – but he also knew it was unlikely the dreamers would be equipped with the means to bring him down. Based on what he'd seen, the dreamers had been armed only with digging implements.

No, his biggest problem was the trees. If the dreamers were in a particularly dense part of the forest, the tree canopy over the digging area might be too thick for him to penetrate. But that was an obstacle he would deal with if and when he came to it.

As it turned out, he didn't have to deal with it. Although the forest was home to occasional clusters of densely packed conifers and moon-pines, because of the sub-zero temperatures and the limited amount of light on Trenzalore, the trees that populated it were, for the most part, sickly, spindly and widely spaced. Most of the growth was at ground level, and involved species of plants that had adapted to the harsh conditions: moss, ferns, fungi. These coated the forest floor in a thick, straggling carpet, which sometimes made progress difficult – and as a result, those townsfolk who *did* occasionally have reason to enter the forest tended to stick to tried and trusted paths.

The section of forest where the dreamers had gathered, about two miles on from where Tomalin Pilke stood guard, was off the beaten track but only lightly populated with stunted and denuded trees. As the whirligig chugged overhead, the Doctor looked down to see the dreamers gathered below – who, in turn, all stood holding their various digging implements, staring up at him. Eerily they all wore the same expression on their otherwise blank-eyed faces – a seething and entirely alien rage. For a moment it was as though the faces of the townsfolk had become transparent; as though he could see through them to the alien infiltrator beneath.

As he had done with Tomalin, he raised his hand in a cheery wave.

'Hello there!'

There was a sound like escaping gas as the dreamers, in unison, bared their teeth and hissed at him.

'Not very friendly,' he muttered, though in truth the reception neither surprised nor concerned him. He was already assessing the terrain, his eyes scanning the area that the dreamers had excavated.

There was a large rectangular crater in the earth, blacker than the foliage that surrounded it, but he couldn't see what it contained. 'Damn these old eyes,' he murmured, and made an adjustment to the sonic, decreasing the oscillation of the whirling blades and sinking slowly towards the earth. As he descended, carefully negotiating a route through the few trees that stretched up towards the night sky, the dreamers became agitated. They clustered beneath him, the more agile leaping up, clawed hands swiping the air like cats confronted with a dangling ball of wool.

The Doctor remained out of reach. He descended just low enough to see into the pit they had dug.

Something white glimmered in the dark soil. A human skeleton, rags still clinging to its mottled bones. From the looks of it, it had been there for many years. What could an alien invader want with a long-dead corpse?

The Doctor was more apprehensive than puzzled, though. From his travels he knew that mortal remains could sometimes be far more than they appeared. He had come across many cadavers – and several skulls – over the centuries that had turned out to be receptacles for powerful alien energies.

'Who's your friend?' he called, not really expecting an answer.

He didn't get one. The dreamers continued simply to hiss and claw at him.

The Doctor considered trying to appeal to them, to break through the alien influence controlling them, warn them that mysterious skeletons buried in woods never boded well...

But he didn't. There was no point. Instead he spoke directly, and mockingly, to whatever lurked behind their eyes.

'Still too scared to face me, are you? Still prefer to skulk in the woods, playing with your glove puppets and messing about with old bones?' He shrugged.

'Frankly, I'm disappointed. In fact, you're such a rubbish enemy I'm almost embarrassed to be talking to you.' He consulted his watch. 'And ooh, look, it's nearly time for tea and biscuits. I'm not missing that for anyone. So when you do decide to come out of hiding, look me up and we'll have a chat. But I warn you, all the Jammy Dodgers may well be—'

That was when the first rock hit him.

The Doctor didn't see who had thrown it. It simply hurtled up from below and whacked him on the leg.

Fortunately it was his wooden leg, and it did no more than make a hefty *clunk* before ricocheting off.

'Oi!' he said indignantly. 'Watch it. You'll chip the varnish.'

Another rock whizzed towards him, and this time he made a hasty mid-air manoeuvre to avoid it, which caused him to sway from side to side. This second rock was so close he felt the breeze of it as it flew past his nose.

Time to go, he decided, knowing that if a rock did clonk him on the head and knock him out he'd plummet to the ground. Unfortunately the whirligig wasn't all that nifty. Before getting it to ascend, the Doctor first had to stabilise the rocking motion, which required several fiddly adjustments on the sonic... by which time, more missiles – not just rocks, but spades, hoes and picks – were flying up towards him.

Most missed, or fell short, but not all. There was a *clonk* as another projectile hit his wooden leg. And then a rock or a lump of wood rebounded off his (fortunately heavily-padded) shoulder, eliciting an 'oof' of pain.

But these were merely minor flesh wounds. He was far more concerned when a hoe, hurled like a javelin, shot past him and into the spinning blades of the whirligig.

With a horrible crunching sound, the blades slowed, jerked, jammed. 'Whoa!' the Doctor yelled as he felt himself plummeting towards the earth. Then the blades shredded and spat out the bits of wood and metal, and the Doctor was plucked upwards again, as though on a piece of elastic. Frantically he tried to stabilise the machine with the sonic and, although he managed it, it was clear that the whirligig had been damaged. It was making an alarming noise – somewhere between a grinding clank and a feeble *phut-phut-phut* – and although it was still rising, and moving more or less in the direction he wanted it to go, he couldn't help feeling that it was now *limping* through the air.

'Come on, old girl,' he murmured in the same coaxing tone he had long ago used with his TARDIS. 'You can do it.'

He squeezed the sonic hard, pressing its burbling green head to the chunky circular belt buckle in which the motor was housed. The whirligig responded by slowly, stutteringly, making its way over the tops of the trees and back towards the twinkling lights of Christmas.

Once he had made it past the tree line, the Doctor began to breathe more easily. Although the whirligig was still slowing down and losing height, from here it was simply a case of negotiating the few fields and local tracks that lay between the woods and the town. The machine had descended to no more than six metres above the ground, and was chugging along like a car on its final reserves of fuel, when, with a final screeching grind of metal, it gave up the ghost.

Although he didn't exactly crash to earth, the Doctor

made a more rapid descent than he would have liked. He braced his old bones as the ground rushed up to meet him, and the next moment he was tumbling, sprawling, spinning, the lightweight blades attached to the home-made rotor on his back splintering away as he did so.

He came to a halt, lying on what remained of the backpack, which had cushioned his fall somewhat, and facing back the way he had come. Various parts of his body ached, but he didn't think he was *too* badly hurt. He might have to give his coat and trousers a bit of a dust when he got back, though.

He sat up with a groan – and immediately became aware of something moving towards him along the track. Although it was dark, it was coming rapidly and with obvious intent. The Doctor turned on his sonic, using it as a torch.

By the sonic's green light, he saw Tomalin's avid face surging towards him. The young man's eyes had become yellow orbs with black slits for pupils; his lips had drawn back and his teeth were bared, saliva drooling from them. He was clutching the rake so tightly that his knuckles were as white as bone.

Using all the authority he could dredge from his battered body, the Doctor roared, 'Stop!'

But Tomalin didn't stop. He kept on coming. The Doctor tried to push himself to his feet as the possessed man raised the rake above his head for the killing blow.

Then a voice rang out from the darkness behind the Doctor:

'You heard what the Doctor said, boy. Back away!'

All at once the Doctor was being pulled to his feet as bodies surged past him to confront Tomalin. The Doctor looked up into Fergin Eggleton's round, bewhiskered face.

'Got a few bodies together. Thought you might need some help.'

The Doctor nodded his thanks and turned to face Tomalin, who was being held at bay by a posse of villagers bearing a selection of makeshift weapons.

'Don't hurt him,' the Doctor called. 'He's not responsible for his actions.'

Tomalin's head snapped round to regard the Doctor. His eyes were still yellow.

'Tomalin,' the Doctor said in an almost conversational tone, 'why don't you show us your arm?'

Tomalin recoiled as if stung. Hissing at the Doctor he backed away.

'What's wrong with his arm, Doctor?' Fergin asked.

'I think it bears a mark.' The Doctor raised his voice. 'Am I right, Tomalin?'

Instead of replying, the young man hissed once more, then turned and fled into the darkness.

A couple of townsfolk prepared to give chase, but the Doctor held up a hand.

'Let him go.'

Chapter 4

'Tell me about the skeleton.'

Sitting beside the fire in Vida Clatterly's cluttered cottage, the Doctor leaned forward until his chin was resting on the hand curled around the head of his stick. Vida, Christmas's oldest resident apart from himself, and prime keeper of the town's history – an oral tradition passed down through the generations – avoided his eye. Instead she busied herself with the pot of herbal tea that sat on the low table between them, muttering to herself as she stirred it with unnecessary vigour.

She was a small, wizened woman with chestnut-brown skin and large, soft, smoky-grey eyes. She wore a brightly coloured shawl and headscarf, both of which sparkled with a profusion of sequins and buttons. The Doctor had known her since she was a baby; indeed, he had helped deliver her. She picked up a plate piled with irregular, doughy lumps studded with raisins and thrust it towards him.

'Rock cake?'

'Vida,' the Doctor said warningly.

She sighed, her gaze shifting to something dangling

beside the fireplace. It was a metal disc onto which letters had been etched, attached to a frayed piece of ribbon.

'Do you remember giving me that?'

'I remember *making* it,' said the Doctor. 'Christmas under-16s Ice Skating Champion. I forget the year, but I'll never forget your Triple Salco. Now, about this skeleton…'

A deeper sigh this time. 'It's Christmas's greatest shame.'

'Tell me.'

For the first time she met his eyes. 'How long have you been here, Doctor?'

He wrinkled his nose. 'Seven hundred years, give or take a decade or five.'

'The skeleton has been there for nine hundred. I'm one of only three people who know – *knew* – about him.'

'Who was he?'

Vida gazed into the fire, as if she could see the story unfolding there. 'His name was Jalen Fellwood. He was one of the first settlers, a village headsman in the days before the Truth Field. He was… a bad man. Some say he was in league with dark forces. He took a young bride, a girl called Summerly Treece, and murdered her as a sacrifice to the evil he worshipped, in the hope that in return he would be granted untold powers. But Summerly's father, Rolan, another headsman, gathered a party of 'righteous men' to hunt Fellwood down. They pursued him into the woods, killed him and buried his body in an unmarked grave. The ground was sown with salt to prevent his spirit from coming back to take revenge on them.'

'Salt,' the Doctor murmured.

'It's a magical defence.'

'Yes, I know.'

Vida glanced at him. His brow was furrowed. 'You don't think…'

'What?'

She laughed nervously. 'Well… magic doesn't really exist, does it?'

The Doctor leaned back with a grunt. Softly he said, 'That depends how you define it. There are some races so ancient that their science appears to be a form of magic – the Daemons, the Osirans, the Carrionites, the Hervoken…' He smiled, as if with nostalgia. 'And belief is important. The mind is a powerful thing.'

'All the same—' she began, but was interrupted by a knock on the door.

'Come in,' called the Doctor before Vida could say anything.

The door opened and Fergin's chubby face appeared. 'Sorry to interrupt…'

'What is it, Fergin?'

'Just thought you ought to know, Doctor. They're back. Them that went into the woods. And they've brought a bloomin' skeleton with 'em.'

The Doctor entered the Christmas Tavern to find that every member of Fergin's posse had answered his call to arms. Carrying his walking stick in one hand and a hessian sack in the other, he looked round at the rows of faces and saw they bore a myriad of expressions: expectancy, anxiety, fear, determination.

These were good people. Noble people. The Doctor loved each and every one of them.

He sat down and began to talk.

'What we're up against,' he said, 'isn't out there…' he waved his stick towards the window '… it's inside us; or rather, it's inside your loved ones – *our* loved ones. It's inside those who've been dreaming. It's using their bodies as a shield. And that means the only way we can defeat it is to draw it out. And the only way we can do *that* is to incapacitate its hosts.'

There was a murmur of consternation. A question came from the back of the room:

'How do we do that, Doctor?'

'With these.'

The Doctor dumped the sack on the floor, the top, which he had been clenching tight with his fist, falling open. The townsfolk eyed the sack warily as the contents shifted, clattering softly. Fergin reached down and plucked out a silver bauble, a profusion of which decorated the many trees scattered around the town.

'What are they – apart from what they look like?'

The ghost of a smile touched the Doctor's wrinkled lips.

'Bombs.'

Fergin looked at the bauble aghast, as if it might go off at any moment. Disbelief jagged and spiked around the room.

'*What?*'

'*You're joking!*'

'*If you think I'm blowing up our Tareena—*'

The Doctor held up his hands. 'Come on, you lot, you know me better than that. What question *should* you be asking?'

A short-haired girl, whose face wore one of the most

fiercely determined expressions in the room, stepped forward. 'What *kind* of bombs are they, Doctor?'

The Doctor grinned. 'Brilliant! Give that girl a toffee apple!' With a grunt of effort he leaned forward, plucked one of the baubles from the sack and tossed it in the air.

'They're sleep bombs. So here's the plan. We go in, chuck them, the baubles break, gas comes out. When everyone's asleep we nick the skeleton.'

He spread his hands, as if to receive applause.

'And that's it?' said Fergin.

The Doctor looked nonplussed. 'What do you mean, *that's it?*'

'Well, it's a bit… simple.'

The Doctor wagged a finger. 'First rule of saving the universe, Fergin – never come up with a complicated plan. Do that and people forget stuff, things go wrong.'

'What does this… thing want the skeleton for, Doctor?' asked the short-haired girl.

'Ha!' said the Doctor. 'Another excellent question! You're on fire today, Clara!'

The girl rolled her eyes. 'My name's Taskia, Doctor.'

'Course it is. Don't let anyone tell you different.' The Doctor swept his gaze around the sea of faces, as if to ensure they were all listening. 'The skeleton is all that remains of a very bad man called Jalen Fellwood. If I'm right – and I usually am – the Mara will use it as the focal point it needs to become manifest.'

'The Mara?' said Taskia. 'Is that the name of the thing we're up against?'

'Yes.'

'What do you mean, "become manifest", Doctor?' asked Fergin. 'You mean it'll bring the skeleton alive?'

'It'll use it as a framework. It'll put flesh on the bones. Eventually it'll gain sufficient power to adopt its true form.'

'What *is* its true form?' Taskia asked.

The Doctor flapped a hand in the air as if conducting an orchestra. 'Well, strictly the Mara is a gestalt entity. It has many forms, and also none. It comes from the dark places of the inside – or so the Kinda used to say.'

'The Kinda?'

'Never mind. Point is, when it wants to make an entrance, when it's *really* showing off, the Mara becomes a big red snake... well, more cerise, really.' He raised his eyebrows, unimpressed. 'Personally I think it's got inferiority issues.'

Taskia leaned forward and touched his hand, as if to keep him focused. 'So what do we do with the skeleton when we've got it, Doctor? And how will we defeat the Mara?'

The Doctor scowled. 'Questions, questions. Let's just deal with one problem at a time, shall we?'

'You mean you don't know?'

'Well... not yet,' he admitted, and then his saggy, wrinkled face broke into a disarming grin. 'But when it comes to it, I'm sure we'll work *something* out.'

Chapter 5

'There are only two of them,' Fergin hissed into the Doctor's ear. 'We can take them easy.'

He was referring to the sentries, who were standing guard, one armed with a hoe, the other with an axe, outside the door of a large barn. The barn was attached to a farmhouse on the western edge of Christmas, set apart from the community by the snow-covered fields that surrounded it. The farm belonged to the Svorsen family, and indeed, Clem Svorsen, the oldest of the farmer's three sons, was one of the sentries.

The Doctor, peering out from behind a thick hedge, the rest of Fergin's posse crammed into the shadows behind him, shook his head.

'Those boys are friends of yours – friends of all of ours. I won't see them getting hurt – or anyone else for that matter.'

A sullen voice from within the crowd piped up: 'But they're helping the Mara.'

The voice was shouted down, albeit quietly, by some, but there were just as many mutters of consent. The Doctor responded with a fierce hiss.

'They're not *helping* the Mara, they're being *controlled* by the Mara. Those boys, and everyone in that barn, are *victims*, and any one of you could easily be among them. Don't forget that.'

He turned and glared. Several people lowered their eyes in shame.

'How will we get past them then, Doctor?' Fergin asked. 'Distract them somehow?'

The Doctor tapped the side of his nose. 'You leave that to me.'

As soon as the sentries spotted him, strolling out of the snowy darkness, they stiffened and adopted a combat stance, knees bent, legs apart, weapons pointed in his direction.

The Doctor raised a hand. 'Relax, boys, I come in peace. I'm here to speak to the boss.'

Up close he could see how the Mara's influence was affecting the two men. Their skin was red and mottled, as were the whites of their eyes, and even their teeth. He couldn't see the tell-tale marks of the Mara on their forearms because of the bulky jackets they wore, but he suspected they were there: red, curving strips of inflamed skin, which, in time, would become more defined, more snake-like, until eventually they would push their way to the surface and break away, physical offshoots of the Mara itself, infecting whoever they touched.

Abruptly Clem Svorsen's eyes changed. They became yellow, snake-like, the pupils lengthening into black, vertical slits. He opened his mouth and spoke in a voice utterly unlike his own – thin and sinuous, devoid of warmth.

'We *will* talk, Doctor, in time – but not yet.'

'Oh no,' the Doctor said, shaking his head, 'you don't come here and start shouting the odds. This is *my* home, *my* rules.'

The Mara chuckled icily. 'For the most feared man in this universe you are a puny, ineffectual creature. You can't hurt me, Doctor. If you try, you will only hurt those you love.'

'Love?' the Doctor sneered. 'What do you know about love?'

'I read it in the mind of this creature. He has such love for you. They all do. And you for them.'

'Yeah, well, that's what happens when people play Twister in sub-zero temperatures. They stick together. Sometimes literally.'

'Your inane babbling is meaningless, Doctor.'

'That's only if you *think* of it as inane babbling. Me, I call it clever verbal misdirection.'

With that the Doctor withdrew the hand he had sneaked into his coat pocket, opened it out flat and blew on it. A cloud of white dust, like a flurry of snow, engulfed the heads of the two sentries. They coughed and spluttered for a moment, and then, recovering, they glared at the Doctor and raised their weapons.

The Doctor stepped back, hoping he hadn't misjudged the strength of the dosage…

He hadn't. All at once the faces of the men went slack, their eyes closed and they crumpled to the ground.

Turning towards the hedge that bordered the path leading up to the barn, the Doctor spread his hands. 'Ta da!'

Immediately figures emerged and flowed towards

him, dark against the snow. Fergin looked at the unconscious sentries.

'They all right?'

'Sleeping like babies. Not bad what you can knock up at a moment's notice.'

The sentries were dragged out of the way, and then the Doctor stood back as the townsfolk, led by Fergin, hurled themselves against the huge double doors of the barn. The doors shuddered and creaked, but they didn't give. They had evidently been secured from the inside, probably by a thick plank of wood stretched between the doors.

'Hurry!' the Doctor urged, though he knew the townsfolk were doing their best.

Suddenly there was an almighty crack and the doors sagged inwards.

'Almost there,' Fergin shouted, his round face red and sweaty despite the cold. 'One more time! All together…'

The townsfolk surged towards the doors. There was another splintering crack, and abruptly the doors flew open. Taken by surprise, some of the townsfolk fell over, and were quickly hauled back to their feet. The Doctor, standing off to one side, could see a flickering blue-white glow shining out from the barn's interior, and hear a low, thrumming crackle. Some of the townsfolk drew back, awe and fear on their faces. Now that they had gained entry, they looked uncertain how to proceed, heads turning for guidance towards the Doctor. As fast as his creaking joints and wooden leg could carry him, the Doctor hobbled forward.

Like most barns, this one was a huge open space filled with straw and tools. At the far end, on a makeshift bier, was the skeleton of Jalen Fellwood. Surrounding it in a rough circle, lying on their backs like the notches on the edge of a clock face, were the townsfolk who had succumbed to the Mara's influence. They appeared to be having a communal dream, their bodies jerking and shuddering, their eyes rolling beneath their closed eyelids.

The blue-white light was coming from the crackling threads of energy that appeared to be flowing directly from the minds of the dreamers and into the skeleton. From afar the effect was like that of a giant, glowing spider, with the skeleton as the creature's body and the threads of energy as its arched, tapering legs.

Fergin looked at the Doctor, bewildered. 'Shall we throw the sleep bombs now, Doctor?'

Angrier with himself than anyone, the Doctor snapped, 'What would be the point? We're too late!'

The skeleton was effulgent, pulsing with light. The Doctor produced his sonic screwdriver and switched it on, half hoping to disrupt the energy waves, but it was no use. Already the dream-energy was too sustained, too powerful. Shielding his eyes, the Doctor hobbled closer to the dreamers and the skeleton, still grimly adjusting the settings on his sonic.

But he could see through the glow that worm-like threads of membrane were already crawling over the bones, that muscles and veins and organs were forming out of nothing. Moving closer he felt an unpleasant tingling in his skin. Taking a deep breath he stepped into the energy field and immediately cried out. There was a crack, a sharp flash of pain, and he was flung backwards.

Next thing he knew, townsfolk were crowding around

him, pulling him to his feet, asking if he was all right. The Doctor nodded impatiently, turning his attention back to the skeleton. His eyes widened. The townsfolk gasped; some began to back away.

On the bier the skeleton of Jalen Fellwood slowly sat up. It turned its head to regard them.

It was still incomplete, its eyes glaring from their sockets, its musculature visible beneath a ghostly patina of still-forming skin. However, it was clear that the body taking shape around the bones was not human – not entirely anyway. The eyes were those of the Mara, yellow and reptilian. And the skin forming over the flesh was scaly and ridged, darkening to a deep, angry red as they watched.

'What shall we do, Doctor?' asked Fergin, sidling up to him.

The Doctor considered the options; there weren't many. 'As soon as the Mara becomes manifest, throw the sleep bombs. Pass the word.'

Fergin nodded. 'Will that stop it?'

The Doctor's face was grim. 'It's worth a try.'

They didn't have long to wait. Already the human-Mara hybrid was almost complete. It rose from the bier and stretched, luxuriating in its new form. Its head was flat, its snout elongated; a cobra-like collar swelled out on either side of its pale, ridged throat. It opened its mouth to hiss at them, revealing a black forked tongue and curved fangs.

As soon as the blue-white threads of energy between the dreamers and the Mara dwindled and snapped, the Doctor shouted, 'Now!'

A rain of silver baubles flew towards the Mara,

smashing open as they hit the ground. White powder billowed up in a cloud, obscuring the creature. The Doctor narrowed his eyes and held his breath, hoping against hope…

But then he heard a swift, slithering scrape, and next moment he saw a flash of red as the Mara shot sideways, towards the left-hand wall.

There were shouts, screams, pointing fingers. More like a spider than a snake, the Mara scurried up and across the vertical wall. It moved like lightning. Before anyone could move to intercept it, it had slithered up and across the wall and out of the open door.

The Doctor spun round on his wooden leg and hobbled in pursuit. But by the time he had pushed his way through the crowd and was outside, scanning the perpetually snowy landscape, the Mara was nowhere to be seen.

'Any change?'

Samanda Glyde turned from the patient she had been examining. The Doctor was standing in the doorway, leaning on his stick, looking glumly up and down the two rows of hospital beds.

The Christmas infirmary was a wooden building, not much bigger than an average-sized barn, and every bed in its one and only ward was currently occupied. Although this wasn't unusual in itself (after each alien incursion there were nearly always casualties to deal with), what *was* eerie was that these particular patients were so quiet. Samanda's best friend, Taskia, had been at the Svorsens' barn yesterday and had told her what had happened. Since then the alien, the Mara, had not been seen. The tension in the town was palpable, the community enveloped in an atmosphere of brooding apprehension. In the meantime it was Samanda's job to look after the Mara's victims.

Not that they needed much looking after. They were all sleeping peacefully. Part of the reason was because the Doctor had made them all 'dream inhibitors', funny little devices of metal and wire, which he had cobbled together from bits and pieces he kept in the Clock Tower. *Because* he had cobbled them together all the 'dream inhibitors' were different, though they all had one thing in common: activated by a blast from the Doctor's sonic screwdriver, they gave off a steady, bleeping pulse that the Doctor had assured Samanda would keep the Mara out.

Shaking her head in response to the Doctor's question, she said, 'No, they're all still asleep. That's good, isn't it?'

'Yes. And no.' The Doctor hobbled along the central aisle, peering grimly at one sleeping form after another. The faces of the Mara's victims were mottled and red, and on each of their arms was a raised, snake-like mark.

'Why no?' asked Samanda.

'Because they're the eyes and ears of the Mara, and until it's destroyed I can't take the risk of waking them up. But the longer they sleep the weaker they'll become, until…'

'They die,' murmured Samanda.

The Doctor said nothing.

'How will you find it?' Samanda asked.

The Doctor sighed. 'Oh, I expect it'll find me. I don't want to be a show-off, but I'm who it's here for.'

His lined features creaked into a watery smile and his eyes softened. 'In the meantime, how about some hot chocolate? Six sugars in mine.'

Before Samanda could reply the door to the ward opened again and Taskia stood there. She was wide-eyed and her shoulders were heaving, as if she had been running.

'It's here,' she panted. 'That thing… It's in the school.'

Instantly the Doctor's face darkened. He lifted his stick and slammed it down so hard Samanda half expected the floorboards to splinter beneath it. 'Don't you dare!' he roared. '*Don't you dare!*'

For an old man with a wooden leg, the Doctor could move incredibly quickly when riled. He left townsfolk trailing in his wake as he stomped along the main street, flakes of snow settling on his shoulders and in his wispy mane of hair. He halted outside the schoolhouse – a white-painted clapboard building with a blue door and blue windowsills.

'Come out and face me, Mara!' he yelled, waving his stick. 'Come and pick on someone your own size!'

For a moment nothing happened. Then a gasp rose from the cluster of townsfolk ten metres behind him.

'Up there, Doctor! On the roof!'

The Doctor looked up. Sure enough there was the Mara-human hybrid, crouched on the roof of the school, its red flesh a startling contrast to the snow-laden trees behind it. With its mouth open and its fangs bared it seemed to be grinning maliciously.

'What's the matter, Mara?' the Doctor shouted. 'Too scared to face me, man to reptile?'

The door of the school suddenly flew open and what appeared to be the entire population of the town's children streamed out. There were screams and cries of shock from the townsfolk gathered behind the Doctor, many of whom were parents of those among the emerging throng.

The Doctor's face was stony with rage as he scanned the features of the children. Every one of them was now a servant of the Mara. Their faces were flushed, their expressions blank, their eyes staring straight ahead. Those whose forearms were exposed bore the mark of the Mara on their skin.

'Using children to fight your battles now?' he snarled, glaring up at the snake-creature. 'Even for something that spends most of its time on its belly, that's low.'

The children came to a halt in a rough semi-circle. One of them stepped forward. The Doctor recognised him as Aliganza Torp's son. What was his name? Barnable? No, Pericles, that was it.

The boy blinked and suddenly his eyes turned yellow, snake-like.

'Speak your name, Doctor,' he said in a voice like splintering ice.

'Why should I?' the Doctor snorted.

'Because if you don't I shall harm the ones you love.'

The Doctor shrugged. 'Not a very persuasive argument. See, if I tell you my name, all hell – literally – will break loose, and the people I love will die anyway, swept aside like chaff in the biggest storm this universe has ever seen.' He jabbed his stick not at Pericles, but at the snake-creature on the roof. 'But that's what you want, isn't it, Mara? That's what you get off on? You want to stuff your reptilian cheeks with all that barbarity and degradation and cruelty. Cos that's what you are – a bottom feeder, a low, crawling thing upon the earth. You're no benefit to anyone but yourself – so why don't you go back to where you came from, *before I get really cross?*'

He bellowed these last few words, his body shaking with such rage that the townsfolk behind him shuffled back another metre or so.

The Mara, however, was unmoved. It regarded him coldly through the eyes of the small boy it had selected as its spokesman.

Finally it said, 'At least in war the deaths of those you love will be swift. But how much harder will it be to watch the children destroy the parents?'

All at once the motionless children jerked into life. Their eyes turned yellow, and acting as a single entity they opened their mouths and hissed.

As they surged forward, fingers hooked into claws, the Doctor turned and yelled, 'Time to retreat! To the snow farm, like I told you!'

The townsfolk needed no further bidding. Although many of them ached to rush to their children, scoop them up, save them in some way, they trusted the Doctor implicitly and had listened carefully to what he had told them the day before.

The snow farm on the edge of town, with its huge iron gates and its thick stone walls, was to be their refuge, their sanctuary.

As one, with the Doctor hobbling behind them, they turned and ran.

Chapter 6

'Hurry, Doctor!'

Fergin was standing on the inside of the massive gates of the snow farm, his hands curled around two of its metal uprights. With one gate already secure, he was making ready to slam the other, just as soon as the last of the townsfolk were through.

The last in this instance was the Doctor, who, despite his age and infirmity, was still managing to keep ahead of the pack.

He came beetling across the snowy ground, head down, his wooden leg swinging in an arc with each loping step, his walking stick more or less operating as an extra limb.

'Now, Fergin!' he shouted as he hurled himself through the gap.

As a couple of people rushed forward to catch the Doctor before he could fall headlong, Fergin slammed the gate shut. Taskia immediately sprang forward with a heavy chain, which she looped through the two gates, then secured with a fist-sized padlock.

Pericles Torp, leading the group of children, threw

himself at the gate with a furious hiss and tried to scale it, but slid back to the ground.

Placed back on his feet by the townsfolk who had caught him, the Doctor limped towards the gates. He and Pericles glared at each other through the bars for a moment. Then the Doctor spoke.

'All right, Mara, listen to me. I don't take kindly to threats, but I'm prepared to offer you a deal as long as you leave my friends alone. Meet me on the main street in ten minutes, just you and me, face to face. What do you say?'

Pericles blinked his yellow snake eyes. 'What trickery is this?'

'No trickery. Just a chat. But keep the children out of it. Send them back to school. It's the organ grinder *I* want to speak to. Not his monkey.'

The small boy stared at him unblinkingly as the Mara considered the request. Finally it said, 'Very well. But remember, Doctor, the children are beholden to me. I can order them to tear one another apart at a moment's notice.'

The Doctor's eyes narrowed. 'Ten minutes,' he repeated.

Then without another word he turned and limped away.

The Doctor stood alone in the snow, seemingly oblivious to the flakes settling in his hair and on the shoulders of his overcoat. The houses that lined both sides of the wide street were silent, though soft amber light glowed in some of the windows. The Doctor's stance was casual; he looked neither apprehensive nor determined, but merely patient, as if he could wait for hours. A snippet from an old rhyme ran through his mind: *not a creature was stirring, not even a mouse…*

But something *was* stirring. In the swirling white darkness at the end of the street there was a suggestion of movement. A flash of red.

The Mara was coming.

Although it moved on two legs, it seemed to slither from the darkness. It looked more elongated, more snake-like, than it had when the Doctor had seen it in the barn, but it was still recognisable as human. That was good, because it meant that the creature was not yet fully manifest, that its hold on this world remained tenuous. It regarded the Doctor, its eyes shining like yellow lamps, its thin black tongue flickering. Its red scales seemed to pulse, causing its cobra-like hood to flare on either side of its throat like a sail.

Casually the Doctor said, 'Hello, Mara.'

The Mara circled him, its movements lithe, balletic, as if it wished to examine him from every angle. The Doctor remained motionless, staring straight ahead.

When the Mara had circled him entirely and they were face to face again, it said, 'Do you still not fear me, Doctor?'

The Doctor shrugged. ''Fraid not. Sorry. Only those with something to live for feel fear.'

The Mara sounded almost surprised. 'Are you really so weary of life?'

'I've seen the future.' The Doctor grimaced. 'It ends in fire.'

'How delicious,' hissed the Mara. Its tone changed, became less playful. 'You have something to offer me?'

The Doctor nodded. 'Yes. Last-chance deal. Get off this planet, go back to where you came from, and I won't destroy you.'

The Mara threw back its head and laughed. 'Oh, how pitiful. I was hoping for so much more.'

'That's life,' said the Doctor.

Suddenly the Mara lunged towards him, mouth open, fangs glistening. The Doctor stood his ground. When they were almost nose to nose, the Mara halted, looking deep into his eyes. Sibilantly it said, 'You cannot win this battle, Doctor. If you do not speak your name willingly I will *make* you speak it. These people are mine. I can invade their dreams, control them at will. And soon I will invade *your* dreams too. I will crawl through your mind and pluck out your name… and then there will be chaos.'

The Doctor rolled his eyes. 'Yeah, yeah, heard it all before. Boring, boring.' He extended a long finger and poked the Mara in its scaly chest. 'If you're gonna do it, why not do it *now*, eh? Why not get it over with? I'll tell you, shall I? It's because you *can't*. It's because you're not strong enough. You haven't even got inside the heads of half of these *puny* humans yet, have you? You're stuck halfway between the dark and the light, between a rock and a hard place.'

The Mara stepped back, stung by his comments. 'We grow stronger all the time, Doctor. Soon nothing will stand in our way.'

'Soon, soon, soon. Yeah, well, maybe I haven't got time to wait that long.'

'You have no choice. You cannot destroy us. We live on the inside.'

'You're not the only one.'

The Mara narrowed its eyes. 'What does that mean?'

Instead of answering, the Doctor raised a hand and waved it in a circle above his head. 'You know what this is? This place? It's a snow farm. It creates extra snow and ships it out to other colonies scattered around the planet. Humans *love* snow. You ever built a snowman, Mara? You ever had a snowball fight? Caught a flake on your tongue and felt it melt?'

'This is irrelevant,' the Mara sneered.

The Doctor sneered right back. 'Irrelevant! Right. You lot always say that. All you power-crazy despots who just want to conquer and destroy. Anything trivial, anything *fun*, is irrelevant. Well, you know what? I bet Jalen Fellwood won't think it's irrelevant.'

The Mara seemed momentarily caught out. 'Jalen Fellwood is dead.'

'Strictly, yes,' said the Doctor, his voice rising. 'And yet he's still in there, isn't he? Inside you? Whatever vile entity he was in league with all those centuries ago kept a little part of him alive. Trapped inside those old bones. A little seething nugget of hate. Because that's how you got here, isn't it? That's what you latched on to? Like calls to like. Jalen Fellwood may be dead, but he's still your focal point. Your beating heart.' He paused. His voice dropped suddenly. 'Your Achilles heel.'

It was clear that the Mara was rattled. It backed away, its yellow eyes sliding left and right, as if it half expected to be ambushed, attacked. The Doctor stepped forward, still talking, pressing home his advantage.

'Do you know what the people of Christmas did after they had buried Fellwood's body in the forest? They sowed the land with salt. They did it so that Fellwood's spirit couldn't come back, so that he couldn't take his revenge.

'Salt. Such a simple thing. So innocuous. And yet Fellwood and the evil controlling him were trapped by it. Stuck below ground for centuries. And do you know why, Mara? Do you know *why* Fellwood was trapped? It's because he *believed*. He believed that salt was powerful and he believed that salt would destroy him…'

The Doctor's voice dropped to a murmur.

'And you *still* believe it, don't you, Jalen? You *still* believe it.'

The Mara said it again, though it didn't sound quite so sure this time. 'Jalen Fellwood is *dead*.'

By way of response the Doctor looked up at the swirling snow and stuck out his tongue.

A flake landed on it. He swallowed it. Smiled.

'*Have* you ever caught a flake in your mouth and felt it melt on your tongue?' he asked again. 'You should try it, Mara. It's one of life's *irrelevant* little pleasures.' Then he smacked his lips. 'Mind you, this snow has a slightly unusual flavour. It tastes… hmm, what is it now?' His face brightened. 'Oh, yes, I know! It tastes *salty!*'

Suddenly the Mara looked alarmed. Its head snapped up to regard the snow tumbling, drifting, swirling from the sky.

'My own recipe!' cried the Doctor triumphantly, pointing his walking stick at the distant chimney, which, from where they were standing, was all that could be seen of the snow farm. 'All the salt that the people of Christmas could lay their hands on. Mix it with the water in the snow chambers, adjust a few controls, and hey presto! Salty snow!' He grinned. 'Whaddya reckon? Think it'll catch on?'

The Mara screamed. Its red, scaly flesh was beginning to hiss and sizzle as flakes of snow touched it. It whirled, spun, but there was no escape. It rounded on the Doctor, its yellow eyes glaring with fury.

'I'll destroy them all! All the children! All the people you love! I'll order them to tear one another apart!'

The Doctor shook his head. 'Oh, I don't think so. I think you've got it all on to keep body and soul together. Look at you, Mara. You're coming apart at the seams.'

It was true. Each individual flake of snow that landed on the Mara was causing its skin to sizzle, to burn, to liquefy. Within moments the snake-creature resembled a red wax candle exposed to immense heat, its physical form breaking down, dissolving. And as it dissolved it shrivelled, melted away, as if it had never really existed at all, except perhaps in a dream.

The Mara thrashed and writhed and hissed for as long as it could, but its struggles became increasingly weaker, more feeble…

Until eventually all that was left of it was a scattering of brittle grey bones on a ground layered with freshly fallen snow.

Aliganza Torp woke with a gasp from what felt like the longest, deepest sleep he had ever had. He thought he might have been dreaming strange dreams, but he couldn't really remember. The first thing he saw when he opened his eyes was the face of an old man peering down at him. He knew the old man, but it took a moment to place him – and then Aliganza realised: it was the

Doctor. The Doctor was holding a strange-looking necklace in his hands, which he appeared to have lifted from around Aliganza's head.

'Hello,' the Doctor said gently. 'Welcome back.'

Aliganza blinked. He had a feeling he wasn't in his own bed. 'Have I been away?'

'In a manner of speaking,' the Doctor said, and dropped the funny-looking necklace into his overcoat pocket.

'What's that?' Aliganza asked.

'What?' And then the Doctor saw where Aliganza was looking. 'Oh, that. It's a dream inhibitor.'

'A dream inhibitor? What does that mean?'

'It means,' said the Doctor, 'no more nightmares.'

Instinctively, Aliganza looked at his forearm. He half expected something to be there, but there was nothing.

A sudden memory of yellow eyes flashed through his mind. His hand shot out and gripped the Doctor's arm.

'Doctor,' he gasped before he knew what he was saying, 'are we safe now? Has it gone?'

'Yes,' said the Doctor soothingly, and patted the hand clutched around his arm. 'It's gone.'

'Forever?' Aliganza asked.

The Doctor paused. He tilted his head to one side.

'Ah, well now,' he murmured, and his wrinkled features crumpled into a crooked half-smile. 'Who can say? Forever is a very long time.'

Available now in the *Time Trips* series:

BBC
DOCTOR WHO

THE DEATH PIT
A.L. Kennedy

Something odd is going on at the Fetch
Brothers Golf Spa Hotel. Receptionist Bryony
Mailer has noticed a definite tendency towards
disappearance amongst the guests. She's
tried talking to the manager, she's even tried
talking to the owner who lives in one of the
best cottages in the grounds, but to no avail.
And then a tall, loping remarkably energetic
guest (wearing a fetching scarf and floppy
hat) appears. The Fourth Doctor thinks he's in
Chicago. He knows he's in 1978. And he also
knows that if he doesn't do something very
clever very soon, matters will get very, very out
of hand…

978 1 448 14184 5

Available now in the *Time Trips* series:

INTO THE NOWHERE
Jenny T. Colgan

The Eleventh Doctor and Clara land on an
unknown alien planet. To the Doctor's delight
and Clara's astonishment, it really is unknown.
It's a planet the Doctor has never seen. It's not
on any maps, it's not referenced on any star
charts or in the TARDIS data banks. It doesn't
even have a name. What could be so terrible
that its existence has been erased?

978 1 448 14183 8

Available now in the *Time Trips* series:

KEEPING UP WITH THE JONESES
Nick Harkaway

Deep in the gap between the stars, the TARDIS is damaged by a temporal mine. It's not life-threatening, but the Tenth Doctor will need a while to repair the damage. But he's not alone. The strangely familiar-looking Christina thinks the Doctor has arrived in her bed and breakfast, somewhere in Wales. In fact, the TARDIS seems to have enveloped Christina's entire town – and something else is trapped inside with it. A violent, unnatural storm threatens them all and – unless it's stopped – the entire universe.

978 1 448 14187 6

Available now in the *Time Trips* series:

SALT OF THE EARTH
Trudi Canavan

The Third Doctor and Jo Grant arrive for a
well-deserved holiday of sun and 'blokarting'
on a salt lake in Australia in 2028. Weird
sculptures adorn the landscape – statues carved
from the salt. People have been leaving them
in the salt lakes for years – but these look
different. Grotesque, distorted figures twisted
in pain. They don't last long in the rain and the
wind, but they're just made of salt...
aren't they?

978 1 448 14188 3

Available now in the *Time Trips* series:

A HANDFUL OF STARDUST
Jake Arnott

The TARDIS is diverted to England in 1572,
and the Sixth Doctor and Peri meet John
Dee – 'mathematician, astrologer, alchemist,
magician, and the greatest mind of our
time'. ('Only of *your* time?' the Doctor asks,
unimpressed.) But what brought them
here? When the Doctor discovers that Dee
and his assistant have come across a 'great
disturbance in the cosmos, in the constellation
of Cassiopeia,' he realises that they are all in
terrible danger.

978 1 448 14185 2